I0669325

**For a limited time, D.N. Leo gives away
Several e-books and audiobooks in the
Multiverse Collection**

**VISIT THE WEBSITE AND CLAIM YOUR
BOOKS**
http://dnleo.com

**THANK YOU FOR READING!
D.N. LEO**

Synopsis

When a fairy tale ends up in a bloodbath, virtue rises.

Dinah isn't just a private investigator, she solves unthinkable mysteries in the multiverse, and has never lost a case until her best friend becomes a victim in a series of mass murders. Someone is toying with the human race and sending threats across the cosmos.

Arik, an Oxford professor in mythology, holds the key to several secrets in the multiverse. When Dinah travels to Earth to seek help from him, they discover one of the secrets he knows could make him the next victim.

As the danger increases, so does their mutual attraction. But fate might have something else in store for them in a twist of a fairy tale.

Dark Solar is an urban fantasy trilogy, full of action, magic, surprises, science and romance. All books are available at http://dnleo.com.

DARK SOLAR TRILOGY

http://dnleo.com

Book 1 - Oleander

Book 2 - Wolfsbane

Book 3 - Maikoa

PART ONE

CHAPTER 1

1980 Dalat, Vietnam

Bridget rushed through layers of steel doors to enter one of the top-security areas in the Tri-Sun headquarters on the outskirts of Dalat, an exotic French settlement in the Vietnam highlands. Fire alarms rang throughout the building. Speakers barked out evacuation commands. Pushing against the stream of people hurrying out, she soon reached an area with no traffic at the center of the building.

In the central hall, she stared at the large staircase leading to the upper level where the executive offices were located. Waves of smoke poured down the stairs. The smell of burned pine, Dalat's signature wood, engulfed the air. A window cracked and broke, the blazing breezes rushing in to fan the flames.

Her high heels would be a hindrance, but she couldn't run through the burning debris without them on, so she lifted the long tail of her long formal velvet dress and hurried up the stairs.

The large landing of the executive level was indeed in flame. The symbol of the three overlapping solar eclipses was displayed prominently in the middle of one of the burning walls in front of her. To her left was a smoke-filled corridor . To her right was a fire exit, leading down.

"Bridget!"

She didn't need to look back to know who was calling her—it was the deep, calm voice of the one person who would always be her constant no matter what life brought her way.

"What are you doing here, Quinn?"

He rushed over and tugged at her elbow. "I should ask you that question. Let's leave before we're both toast."

She pointed at the corridor filled with smoke. "Kane's in there. I can't leave him." The carpet started to catch fire, and the glass in the windows began to crack. Soon the metal window frames would melt, as would the body of anyone walking into that corridor.

"There's nothing you can do now. Please...we can talk outside."

"My husband is in there, and I won't leave him."

"Kane is my best friend. I want to save him, too. But he has no chance of surviving this fire, Bridget. Even if you could get to him, what would you expect to find? His body? Think about your children for God's sake."

"They will be safe in your hands."

"No!"

"Quinn, if our relationship means anything to you, then you will treat my children as your own. Please."

"No, I won't accept this. Our relationship means too much to me. I won't let you go in there to die."

"It's more than my husband's life that I have to save, Quinn. We started this, and we have to finish it."

She turned abruptly and charged toward the corridor. Despite her kicking and screaming, Quinn grabbed her from behind and dragged her toward the exit. He was too strong for her to break free.

"Okay, let me down!" she screamed. "I'll go with you."

He didn't give up and kept carrying her toward the exit. He kicked the exit door open and got them both safely out to the stairwell. She grabbed onto a steel rail on the wall to get her footing and then kicked hard at Quinn. He lost his balance and let go of her. She pushed him away, sending him stumbling down the stairs.

"I'm sorry, Quinn," she said and then ran back into the building, grabbed a broken chair, and jammed the door handle with it.

Through the small window on the door, she saw Quinn trying to break in.

Then behind him came a wave of fire from below.

"Quinn!" she called out and grabbed the door handle. It was so hot it burned her hand to the bone.

Despite the excruciating pain, she yanked the exit door open as another wave of fire blew upward, exploding into the room and knocking her away.

"I'm so sorry, Quinn." She looked down at the burning stairwell, the flames so hot they had melted everything in their way, including metal and concrete.

Knowing Quinn couldn't have survived this fire blast, she wiped away her tears and headed toward the burning corridor that led to the executive wing where her husband would be waiting.

CHAPTER 2

Dinah was flying. This was certainly different, flying with her own wings as opposed to flying with the wings of her weaponry suit. She could feel the cold breeze blowing through every feather, the strong force of wind pushing against her wings and pulling her shoulders back slightly. She felt a sensation in her muscles whenever she flapped her wings. *These angel wings feel great!* she thought.

She wondered if the sensation would be the same once she became used to these wings. Jael was right—simply having angel wings didn't make her an angel, a position she had no intention of taking on. Working for Ciaran in investigative roles—or in anything having to do with chemicals—was what she did best and where she could contribute the most. She believed he would soon promote her to a council of some sort in Eudaiz. She could make a difference in the multiverse by being associated with the most prosperous universe in the cosmos.

In the distance, she could see Arik racing up the hill. He had caught a glimpse of her flying toward him. He must have had a heart attack, waking up and finding she was gone.

He had said he loved her. Dinah couldn't believe it. It had happened too fast and still felt like a dream. A human loved her, even after not only finding out she wasn't human, but also seeing her turn into a monster and rip the heart out of a magical hulk. Jael had told her she wasn't a monster but was possessed by her evil aunty. But Arik didn't know that.

"Dinah!" he called out.

As she watched him glide through the bushes and rush up the hill to her, she was sure she loved him, too. That was an amazing development considering what she understood about her psychological profile and what she was capable of.

She flapped her wings, flew in a circle, and flapped again. Then there was a tearing sound and a thud. She looked up and saw her wings were caught in a large tree, leaving her dangling over the ground.

Arik rushed over, standing on the ground below her. "Dinah, are you okay? Let go of the wings. Come down. I'll catch you."

This had happened before. She'd gotten caught in a tree while flying with her artificial wings. But now she'd discovered the first disadvantage to having real wings was that rubbing them against the spiky tree branches actually hurt. "Let me retract them," she said.

"Come on, Dinah, let go of them." He moved back and forth, adjusting his position to catch her when she fell from the tree.

"You're looking up my dress, Arik."

"I've seen you naked before. Come down here, Dinah!"

"You're such a romantic!" she said then yanked at her left wing. "Ouch." She pulled again. "Ouch!" A couple of feathers floated lazily to the ground. Arik picked them up.

"Dinah, you're bleeding! Stay still. I'll untangle you." He started climbing the tree.

"Don't do that—you're afraid of heights, you silly," she said and pulled hard at both wings. She fell to the ground, landing on her backside. Her wings were retracted halfway and still dropping feathers to the ground.

Arik slid down the tree trunk and darted over to her. He pulled her into his arms and held her so tight she could hardly breathe. She could feel his body vibrating with emotion, making her feel bad for fiddling with her wings and not coming back to him quicker.

"You scared the hell out of me. Where did you go?"

"Jael got me. He said—"

She didn't have time to finish her sentence before he kissed her. And he was a hell of a kisser. Her toes curled, and she thought her wings would, too.

Arik traced his hands up her back to her shoulders. Then he stopped the kiss and looked at her wings. "This isn't a suit!"

"I know. They're real wings."

He smoothed a ruffled feather on the edge of her left wing then kissed her cheek. "You're beautiful."

"Don't you want to know how this came about?"

"Not if you don't want to tell me."

She smiled. "You saw me turn into a monster and kill Roallix. After all that, why did you say you love me?"

"Because I do."

"Even when I turn into a monstrous creature?"

"Do I need to sing a song about it?"

She chuckled. "No. I don't mind your singing, but I can't respond. I'm tone deaf."

He sat down on a stone and pulled her down to sit beside him. "I've told you I don't care what you are."

"How about an angel?"

"What?"

"Jael is my father. And Charmine, the woman on the hill, was my mother. She was pregnant with me at the time."

"And you aren't supposed to come into contact with yourself when you time travel. That's why you were knocked out when you touched her."

She nodded.

"Wait, it was 1864. That makes you..."

She wagged a finger. "Earth age is irrelevant in the multiversal space."

"A woman's age is irrelevant anywhere." He rubbed his hand across her bare shoulders after she had completely retracted the wings. "You must be cold. Let me go get your jacket."

She smiled as she watched his shadow retreating down the rolling hill.

A short while after, a shadow reeled toward her from the opposite direction. She squinted, trying to make it out. It wasn't just any shadow—it was Cooper. She darted toward him. He was covered in blood.

"Cooper!"

He fell into her arms. She lowered him to the ground and lay him gently on the grass.

"Stay with me, Cooper. I'll take you back to the camp. Xanthe is a healer. She'll fix you. Oh no...where's your arm?" she cried out, looking at where his right forearm should have been. It had been cut off above the elbow. He was on the verge of passing out and couldn't respond.

"Arik!" Dinah shouted down the hill, where she could still see a glimpse of Arik's shadow. He didn't hear her. "Arik!" she cried again.

This time, he turned around and raced back up the hill.

"I need to talk to Arik," Cooper said weakly.

"He's coming, Cooper. Don't speak. We'll take you back to the village."

"Where's Arik?"

"He'll be here soon. You've lost too much blood. Please don't speak. Keep your strength." She didn't realize she was weeping.

Arik rushed over. "Cooper, what happened? Where's Jenny?" He reached down the lift Cooper up to carry him, but Cooper resisted.

"Jenny wanted me to tell you that they want you. You're in trouble, Arik."

"Who are they? Where is my sister?"

Cooper passed out before he could answer.

CHAPTER 3

Madeline rolled over to find Ciaran's side of the bed empty and cold. She sat up too quickly, making herself slightly dizzy. They were in a hotel room. This was the most cynical twisted joke fate had played on them since they'd left Earth. Ciaran had run a global pharmaceutical conglomerate before they'd left. He'd had the red carpet laid at his feet wherever he went. But now they had to stay in a downtown hotel like ordinary humans.

She sighed, resigned to the situation. The truth was that, although they were Eudaizians now, once a human, always a human. Her psychic ability wasn't flaring, so that meant Ciaran was fine. Perhaps he'd just sneaked out for a walk.

New York had been her home for thirty-three years. Although she'd had an ordinary life as a journalist, she had so many memories here. The LeBlanc's New York headquarters was the second largest after the one in London. Ciaran must have had many business dealings here and worked with a lot of people. She smiled. Her husband was sometimes much too sophisticated for her liking. He always had stories and theories about everything that had happened in his life. She wondered if there was anything he couldn't explain.

A shadow from inside the room moved past the window only a few feet away from her. She jerked away, startled. But when she looked again, all she saw was the empty corner of the luxurious suite. She shook her head, willing her mind to scan around the room.

Her psychic ability had improved. Most of the time, she could turn it on and off and read the minds of ordinary humans. She respected people's privacy, though, and didn't scan unless it was absolutely necessary.

The signal bounced back. *Empty*. She must be tired.

She walked around the room, contemplating a harder mind scan. If there were any creatures nearby, she'd be sure to pick them up. She had a strange feeling she was missing something, and she didn't like it.

The door slid open, and her gorgeous husband walked in like a god, brightening both the room and her mood. Ciaran LeBlanc—king of Eudaiz, the most prosperous universe in the cosmos, warrior in many battles across the multiverse, and undefeatable predator in his business on Earth—stood there with a paper bag in his hand. He smiled and opened the bag, and she could smell freshly made bagels. She now saw what her psychic ability hadn't allowed her to see.

Damn! It wasn't the food or the fact that she was starving at the moment that made her stomach flutter. It was the twinkle from those striking gray eyes and the killer smile on that God-given face that made her stomach flip and her body quiver with lust.

"Bagels from your favorite bakery on Fifth Avenue, First Councillor. I hope you're happy with the room service."

She stepped up and over to cross the bed, reached up to grab his collar, and yanked him down to the bed. She straddled him and smiled down at him.

"You've crushed your bagels, First Councillor."

She ravished his lips, and he responded hungrily. Her hands slid under his shirt and roamed up his taut torso, caressing each well-defined muscle.

He didn't just lie there and take it. His hands traveled all over her body. No matter how many times they had been intimate or how long they'd been together, he always surprised her. She soon lost track of what they were doing. And then, he did what he did best.

He took control.

When their needs had been sated, she curled into his arms. "Where're my bagels?" she asked.

"I'm sorry to say you've lost your privilege for those bagels. Plus, you've crushed them somewhere beneath us on the bed. I don't think they're edible any longer."

She propped herself up on her elbows and kissed his cheek. "You bought them, so I'll eat them. I don't care how deformed they are."

He chuckled and sat up, finding his shirt and tossing it to him.

She spoke through a mouthful of bagel. "Arik's father is fine. So now, we'll go back to Eudaiz...or do you have other business to see to here?"

He tied back long raven hair that nearly touched his shoulders. She knew he did that when he anticipated action. "He said he was fine on the phone, but I think the explosion was too much of a coincidence. I'm going to visit the site and stop by to see if Diana is okay. He said she was fine, but I don't believe him."

"How will we get there? You wanted to keep a low profile, and you didn't contact your staff. Are we going to take the metro?"

He laughed. "I wouldn't stoop that low, First Councillor. I've arranged transport for us. We'd better go soon—the sight of you eating bagels naked could possibly delay my important business all day long, and then we'll never get home to our children."

She grinned, finished her bagel, and dressed. "What kind of transport? You didn't get a ridiculous sports car, did you? Remember that you want to lay low, my king."

He shook his head and smiled. "Well, it's something on wheels."

Suddenly, a vision flashed at her, hard and fast. She gasped and grabbed the edge of the table to steady herself.

Ciaran held her shoulders. "Madeline, are you okay?" His eyes grew intense, and the smile faded from his face.

She pasted on a smile. "It's nothing!"

"You're as pale as a sheet. It must be something. Are the children okay?"

"Yes, Ciaran. The kids are fine. It wasn't a precognition."

She hadn't given him a satisfactory answer, and he knew it. But she hadn't lied—it hadn't been a precognition.

It was a flashback, and one she didn't want to talk about.

"Are you fine to go with me now, or do you need to rest?"

"I'll go with you."

He nodded. At the door, he stopped and asked again, "Is everything okay?"

"Yes." She smiled and sauntered ahead. She didn't need eyes in the back of her head to know he was frowning at her.

CHAPTER 4

Dinah flew again. This time, she knew the power of her wings and flapped them with strength. Not only did she want to fly away, she wanted to fly to where Cooper was. "Why did you leave, Cooper? I can help you," she said to the wind. She flapped again, and again.

Not only were they business partners, but they had been friends for a long time. Cooper wasn't oblivious to life—or ignorant as he often appeared to be to a lot of people. He cared about her, and she knew that in difficult situations, he was a selfless person. Much of the time, she thought Cooper was a better citizen than she was.

She looked down and saw Arik running below, shouting up at her. He waved his hands, gesturing for her to come down.

She circled in the air and then landed.

Arik rushed over, grabbing her shoulders. "You are not going anywhere or doing anything by yourself. This is Xiilok—not exactly the multiversal safe haven. I understand you're worried about Cooper. I'm worried about my sister, too. Before we left, there was the explosion at my parents' place, and I still haven't been able to get an answer from Ciaran because the device he gave me isn't working. I need you to calm down and help me figure out how to tackle this situation before you take any hasty action."

"Wow, that was a long speech, Arik. I'm sorry I made you worry. I just wanted to try to fly out my frustration. I know we have to come up with a plan."

Arik exhaled his relief and then sat down on a stone. He buried his face in his hands. "I know I can't afford to make mistakes, but I just don't know what to do right now."

"I think we should attack the Red Shield tribe. It's risky, but it's an immediate action we can take. Cooper said the Red Shield have something to do with Jenny being taken. And they're just over the hill."

"He also said the machine that captured Jenny was manmade. Red Shield technology is primitive. I doubt they'd use a machine like that."

"That's an assumption, Arik. In terms of technology, I don't know what humans are capable of. But if there's one thing I know for sure, it's that humans are complicated. They might not have the most sophisticated technology, but if they have an agenda, they can always force space creatures to use their technology."

"Am I supposed to feel flattered just because I'm a human?"

"You're no longer an ordinary human. You're a Xiilok citizen and the up-and-coming leader of the Yellow Shield tribe. You might liberate this universe for a change."

Arik rolled his eyes. "I just want to find my sister. That's all I can think of right now."

"That's why I suggest going to the Red Shield. Do you remember a bunch of Grace lookalike robots and the Red Shield camp? They didn't look very sophisticated. We can get in to see if they have Jenny. I think that's where Cooper would go."

Arik nodded. "All right, but we won't attack directly. And only the two of us will go. I won't take Yellow Shield soldiers there."

"Of course not. If we take soldiers, I want real fighters, not liabilities," she said.

"What exactly are you saying?"

"No offense, Arik, but the soldiers in your tribe have no training."

"The Yellow Shields are peaceful people."

"And that's good when you live in peaceful times. But this is *not* that time."

Arik shrugged.

From the corner of her eye, Dinah saw a shadow creeping away from behind a rock. "It heard us!" she said and flew toward the space creature.

It was the scorpion with spider legs. The size of the creature didn't stop Dinah from pounding on it. After taking a few of Dinah's punches, it dropped a small item from its belly to the ground. Some of its legs were broken, but it tried to retreat on the ones it had remaining.

Dinah picked up the item from the ground. In her palm was a small knife she had made for Cooper. It wasn't a simple knife, but a knife whose blade was coated with the most exotic poison in the cosmos. Cooper would never have left that knife behind. She turned around to look at the creature.

"This is Cooper's," she said. "Did you hurt him?"

The creature tried to scramble away but couldn't move quickly because some of its broken legs dangled and tangled with the unbroken ones.

"I asked if you hurt Cooper?"

She remembered the electronic notepad Cooper had left behind, saying he was sorry about Jenny and wouldn't stop searching until he found her. Was that the last she would ever hear from him? What if he was lying in a ditch in Xiillok somewhere, waiting for her to rescue him?

"Where did you take him? Did you eat him?" She jumped on the creature, stabbing it again and again with the very knife she had given Cooper.

Arik yanked her off the pile of what used to be a space creature.

"You've killed it a thousand times over, Dinah. That's enough. Calm down."

She pulled herself out of his grip and charged at the dead animal again.

"Cooper is a smart guy. He wouldn't die that easily. Look at yourself—even if Cooper is dead, he'll come back to life to be angry at you."

"I don't need to look at myself. I know what I look like."

"No, you don't." He grabbed her and pulled her toward a puddle of muddy water. "Look." He pointed.

She looked down at her reflection in the water.

She saw a face she didn't recognize—pale skin laced with bloody veins, huge dark black eyes. She was unfamiliar with that look, but she knew it was the evil part of her. She withdrew from the water and its reflection.

Arik pulled her into his arms, holding her tight, and whispered into her ear. "Don't be scared. I've seen it before. It's not you. But it seems to take control of you when you lose control of your emotion. If you don't control yourself, it will kill you and those around you. I don't know anything at all about the angel business, so that's the best explanation I can come up with. No matter what causes this, I need you to trust me and know I'll be right next to you." He kissed her cheek.

"Jael told me my evil aunt possessed me and put a curse on me before she died. The evil will come out when I'm weak. But I didn't know it was triggered by emotions, too."

"Now you do."

"My biological profile suggests I don't have human emotions."

"Well, apparently you have them. But that doesn't make you weak."

"I have feelings for you, but I think it's merely a positive chemical reaction. I want to love you the way you love me. But how will that work out if loving you makes me vulnerable to the evil inside me?"

Arik stared at her for a moment. She could see in his eyes that he didn't have an answer for her.

She stood and patted his shoulder lightly. "Let's go find Cooper and Jenny."

CHAPTER 5

Madeline's jaw dropped as Ciaran, looking magnificent in a leather jacket, zoomed up on a giant motorbike to the sidewalk where she stood waiting. She didn't know what sort of bike it was, but the sight of him riding it sent her hormones into frenzy.

Ciaran took his helmet off, grinned, and handed Madeline a helmet. "Would you like to go for a ride, First Councillor?"

"Do you have a license?"

"No, but I can't be fined."

"Because you're king of Eudaiz, or because you're no longer a citizen here?"

"Neither. If they want to give me a fine, they'll have to catch me first."

She was about to hop on the bike when she saw a white van parked across the street. She felt a shiver at the back of her neck.

"What is it, Madeline?"

"Huh?"

"You looked like you had a sensation. Another vision?"

She shook her head. She'd told him before that she hadn't had a precognition, but she knew him too well. He hadn't believed her then and had asked the same question again to try to make her slip with an inconsistency. Her lies would never be consistent because she didn't have a poker face and was downright untalented when it came to lying.

But she had received some strange signals from the white van and then an odd sensation from a flashback she didn't want to remember.

She was confused. The flashback became stronger by the second, bringing a sense of nostalgia and sweet memories.

She was in trouble.

Ciaran wasn't a psychic, but he could see right through her, especially when she was in emotional turmoil. She scanned the street again, looking for the white van. The van was an immediate matter at hand and potentially a danger. She wasn't going to spend a drop of her energy on a silly flashback right now.

She squinted, trying to peek into the mind of the occupant of the van who had sent her the signal.

Buzzing noises.

"The white van across the street," she said. "I'm getting a strange feeling about it."

Ciaran didn't look in the van's direction, and he kept a neutral expression on his face. "Something supernatural?" he asked.

She shook her head. "I'm not sure. I haven't had this sensation before. I'm pretty sure the signal from that van is aiming straight at us. Someone was hoping we would catch it. But I don't know what kind of signal it is." Then, from the corner of her eye, she saw a shadow of her past—someone she thought she would never see again—walking along the street.

"Madeline!" Ciaran called out.

"Huh?"

"Did you see something else other than the van?"

"No, nothing." *Except that person*, she thought. She was sure it had nothing to do with the situation at hand, and especially nothing to do with the van waiting for them across the street, so she brushed the thought away.

She blinked and saw Ciaran's striking gray eyes paused on her face a fraction longer than usual.

Damn, he'd caught her.

He was way too smart for her to lie to. Just after they'd gotten married, he had told her all his secrets, including the unflattering ones. She had done the same. But she'd held one back. This one.

Damn it! She couldn't now go back on her word and say she had forgotten to mention it. Why had she held it back? *Damn it, damn it!* She couldn't think straight right now. A girl was entitled to a few secrets. Maybe. But not Ciaran's girl. And she wasn't just a girl. She was his *wife* and the First Councillor in his Sciphil committee.

"Madeline!"

"Huh?"

"Are you okay?"

"No. I mean, yes. I just couldn't get the signal from that van."

He nodded. "Don't worry about it. Let's go."

She grabbed the helmet and hopped onto the bike. As she did so, she took a quick peek into Ciaran's mind to see what he was thinking.

As she expected, her signal bounced back, empty. He had figured out a way to block her from reading his mind. She sighed. Everyone was entitled to their privacy, and she shouldn't have even attempted it in the first place.

Ciaran drove slowly, checking his rearview mirror to see if the van followed them.

It did. Ciaran accelerated, slowed down, then accelerated again. He drove around the block. The white van followed them wherever he went.

"If you're going to spy on someone, be a little bit more subtle, idiots," Ciaran muttered. "Do you feel the gun in my side pocket?"

Madeline slid her hand under Ciaran's jacket and touched the gun. "Yes."

"That gun is just a normal gun. We'll use it if the situation calls for it. It's not safe for us to show off our supernatural capabilities in the middle of New York, so refrain from turning on your eudqi. That'll also prevent someone from prying information from us."

"So you want us to not only live here like humans but behave like them, too?"

"We can try to behave like humans. But I doubt we can ever be like them again."

Ciaran suddenly slowed down, forcing the white van driver to slam on his brakes and veer around them. When the van drove past, they saw a woman sitting in the front passenger seat. In contrast to the rundown van, the woman was stunning, with long dark hair, emerald eyes, an elegant royal face. She smiled and nodded at Ciaran and Madeline.

Then she turned to the driver and said something to him. The next thing they knew, the van accelerated and zoomed off into the distance, vanishing into the polluted air of New York City.

"Did you get that?" Ciaran asked.

"Yes. You shouldn't have expected any less of me." Madeline smiled and slid the signal gun back into his pocket. "I aimed for the bottom of the car so no one will see the signal system and know they're being tagged."

He smiled at her in the reflective mirror. "Thanks."

As she sat on the motorcycle, her body pressed against his back, she could feel him chuckle. The vibration of his joy was contagious, and it sang through her body.

Red traffic light.

Ciaran stopped.

And then, right in front of her, the shadow of her past walked across the street with the flow of pedestrians.

Other pedestrians pale as his image sparked and floated in halo light. She hoped it was just a vision. But it wasn't. After all these years, he looked just the same. She slammed the helmet visor down and looked away.

CHAPTER 6

Arete frowned at the jar on the table. He couldn't believe he was looking at the primer for inter-world mutation—the golden formula any creature would kill for.   His centuries-long business dealing with Asana had proven its worth after all.

He smiled to himself and leaned back in a chair in the corner of the small dark dungeon in Xiilok. He really shouldn't call it a dungeon. For his business partner, Asana, it was a sacred place of medical and ritual practice.

Regardless of whether he liked it or not, he needed Asana to perform his part well for them both to succeed.

There was a slight noise, and Asana stepped out from a small side doorway.

Hold it together, Arete told himself to stop from laughing out loud when he saw Asana's eyes, his irises swimming with what looked like worms. Having survived the multiverse for a few hundred years, he should have known better than to let mere kids like Cooper and Jenny kick him down the Well of Second Chances.

Arete frowned. *Was that the name of the well*? Recently, his memories had been deteriorating rapidly. He hardly remembered the names of any creatures or locations anymore. That was the curse of being immortal, he figured.

Arete shrugged inwardly. It would work out best for him. Those who drank the water in the well became official shady citizens of Xiilok, the heart of the Amalgam world and the land of the multiversal outlaws. Previously, Asana had kept switching between the Amalgam world and the material world, and at times, he thought Asana would backstab him and take both. But now, Asana had no choice but to compete in the Amalgam world, leaving Arete the freedom to do whatever he wanted.

Arete pasted a smile on his face. "Are you well?" he asked.

"As well as you would expect. You look happy." He pointed his chin toward the jar. "Especially now that you know I have completed the primer."

"How do I know if it works?"

"You don't. You could test it on other creatures, but I made only one dose. I know the formula and can replicate it, of course, but I'm too busy. Now it's your turn to do your part."

"You don't have to worry about that. I told you I'd take care of the material world. I always hold up my end of the business."

"Really? Who did your contractors capture instead of Arik Bonneville?"

"Look, that was a mistake. I didn't know they were that clueless. I gave them clear instructions. But it happened in Xiilok. And you know Earthly creatures are at a disadvantage in Xiilok."

"Yes, I know. They're blind as bats here. But what I don't understand is why you didn't use inter-world mercenaries as you *promised* me. I could have done it myself if I could help it."

"There, that's the problem. You *couldn't* help it!" Arete kicked the chair back and stood up. "Don't point your finger at me. Arik Bonneville is your problem. If you're shitting yourself because he'll be kicking your ass in the Amalgam world, then get your act together. We're getting too close to the date to afford any mistakes. If there's going to be a fight, then get ready for it. It's better to fight the devil you know. The Yellow Shields chose Arik for a reason. If we kill him, and they replace him with someone else, you will be the one to cop the heat—not me."

Arete grabbed the primer jar and turned to leave.

"Are you sure Arik is the only problem I have to deal with?"

Arete smirked. "He's the problem I know of."

"What about the girl?"

"Which girl? Arik's sister? I told you that was a mistake. When my intelligence in the Daimon Gate caught her last name, it sent a signal that confused my people. They thought Cooper was Arik Bonneville—a stupid assumption from Earth mercenaries. But why would they run to the Daimon Gate and declare their names anyway? Was that after they kicked you down the well?"

"What?"

"You heard me! Why did you chase Jenny and Cooper instead of Arik and the other girl? Whatever her name is."

"I ran into them by accident. I didn't chase them."

"Is that right? Okay, my guys didn't take Jenny. I don't know who did, but I don't have her.

Regarding the other girl, my intelligence suggests that she is Eudaizian and working for Ciaran LeBlanc. He has zillions of minions working for him. She shouldn't be a concern."

"Are you sure?"

"Well, no. But anyone and anything to do with Arik Bonneville is an Amalgam world problem. *Your* problem. I have my own shit to take care of. I'll help you this time in exchange for this primer. Otherwise, you're on your own." He raised the jar. "What's in this exactly?"

Now Asana smirked. "Maikoa. The kind that grows in Xiilok."

"The poisonous flower?"

"Don't worry. Although you're an asshole, I still need you. So I'm not going to poison you. But you need to know that one has to die first before mutation becomes possible."

"Well, I'll make sure not to use it unless absolutely necessary. If we get dark solar, there will be no need for this."

Asana nodded. "Let's hope for that!"

As soon as Arete stepped outside the zone encircling Asana's residence and into the shadow of a dimensional shifting rock, he looked around to ensure Asana hadn't followed or sent any creatures after him. Then he opened his palm, revealing a small, shiny talisman. He pressed lightly on the middle of the talisman and waited until it glowed. The voice of the old underworld minor god asked, "Do I need to restrict your calls to three?"

"No, this isn't the underworld, and it's not a fairy tale, either. This is called communication. We're on a mission together. The more we communicate, the better chance we have of achieving what we want. I think we might have a problem with the magical world, the one you're in charge of."

"There are many problems with the magical world, and I am *not* in charge of all of them. Regarding this particular mission, you want me to kill the angel couple. I will do just that. I haven't encountered an issue."

"I need you to make sure there's nothing wrong at your end."

"I just told you everything is fine."

"Umm...do you have someone who can handle the Amalgam world?"

"Maybe. What's wrong with Asana?"

"I think he's on to something."

"You're both always on to something. A coalition of bad guys. What do you expect?"

Arete looked at the jar of primer. "Asana is an expert in poison, isn't he?"

"Yes, so what's your point?"

"I think he's trying to send a mutation potion to the underworld. Your area."

"Why?"

"Well, do you remember a series of explosions in the underworld jails?"

"Yes, those packages were sent from Eudaiz. That's one of the reasons I agreed to help you, because you take on Eudaiz."

"You're mistaken. The packages were sent by Asana. I will defeat Eudaiz and Ciaran LeBlanc. Let me assure you of that. But Asana will always want to take over all worlds. And the underworld is where he tests his mutation potions. He needs an army and slaves, resources he doesn't have at hand."

"Is that right?"

"It might be speculation on my part, but you can check the records of your jail explosions. If you find traces of poison, there is no more I'll have to say. You might know that by reputation, Eudaizians don't do poison."

Silence.

"Why didn't you mention this before? I thought you were allies."

"We're friends until I suspect he's playing tricks on me."

"All right, I'll look into it and will send you someone I think is suitable to replace Asana."

"Thank you." Arete slid the talisman into his pocket and took a last look at the jar of potion. Then he crouched and poured the liquid onto a little tree at the side of the road. The tree shrank, faded in color, and crumbled to the ground, turning into a worm-filled liquid substance. He shook his head. "It isn't mutating into anything, is it, Asana? You must think I'm an idiot." He stood and walked away.

A moment later, the puddle formed into the shape of a long string, then turned into a snake and slithered away.

CHAPTER 7

Charmine returned to her humble quarters, a small hut in the middle of the traveler's land. The term traveler's land might bring terror to many creatures, but for her, it was home.

Travelers of the multiverse had earned many bad names. She didn't know much about the tribe because she had left them a long time ago and had never received a proper education from her mentor. Some called them drifters and some gypsies of the multiverse. They moved from one place to another, and nobody knew their origin. She didn't even know what the term gypsy meant, but she could tell some senior members of the tribe got upset when the name was used to describe them. One thing she knew for sure—the origin of her tribe was elusive, as was their future.

She didn't have any hope that her husband, Jael, would be able to find her here. The traveler's land was harder than Xiilok to find, and even more difficult to navigate through. She sat down at a small table, tracing her fingers over a small woven piece of fabric, one that was supposed to be wrapped around her daughter. Feeling that tears would come, she pushed the fabric away. She refused to believe this was the only reality she had now. There had to be a solution, and once more, she would fight her way out of here.

Then she sensed the familiar presence of her husband. There was nothing more in this universe she longed for at the moment. She rushed toward the door, scrambling over the furniture, some baskets with wildflowers near the door, and a pile of firewood.

This was not the first time she had done this. She'd repeated this action many times, and every single time, she had been disappointed. But without Jael and her daughter, her world didn't make much sense. So she continued to dream and hope—and scramble toward the door whenever she heard a noise.

She yanked the door open, and he was in front of her. The magnificent angel of light stood before her at the door of her humble little hut in the middle of the traveler's land.

She didn't know what to say, and neither did he. It had been days, and she thought this moment would never happen.

He pulled her into his arms. They held each other for a long time, listening to each other's heartbeats. This was the first time since they'd been married by the lake that she'd realized she had to treasure every moment they had together—because they never knew what would happen the next day.

She looked up into his face, twirling a long lock of his sandy hair around her finger. He smiled at her.

He was calm and steady. Always. She was born a traveler, and she traveled constantly. When she'd found him, she thought he would be her constant so that she could stop traveling. It was so ironic what had happened.

"You're real," she said and smiled at him.

"More real than ever. I didn't think I would be able to find you here."

"I know you'd never give up."

He held her hand. "Come with me," he said. "Let's get out of here."

"I promised the leader—"

"I spoke to him. He'll let you leave."

"What did you promise him?"

"I'll tell you later."

"No, Jael. It's been thousands of years, and they have never broken the tradition. What did you promise?"

He smiled and brushed a stray hair from her forehead. "I promised him a home."

"A home? You promised the travelers a home?"

He nodded. "It's a very special home that I can provide. And most importantly, he agreed."

She nodded.

Then he looked into her eyes. "What's wrong, Charmine?"

"I've lost our daughter."

"No, you didn't."

"I don't understand. You haven't even asked if we have a boy or a girl. You haven't even asked where our baby is."

"It's a long story, but I met our daughter in the future. So I know we have a daughter, and she is supposed to be alive until her adulthood."

"In the future?"

"Yes, I used this." He pointed to the bracelet he was wearing. She had an identical one, and she knew what it was. She had been planning to use it for her escape if Jael hadn't found her.

She nodded. "Yes, I know we can travel across dimensions and the world with it."

"The girl who was thrown into the rock when she tried to help you during the hilltop fight was our daughter."

"She was?" She wiped a tear that rolled down her face. "I was pregnant, and she tried to touch me."

"Yes, that's exactly why it happened. You're not supposed to come in contact with yourself when time traveling. I figured that out after you gave birth and your tribe took you away. I asked a lot of people before coming to that conclusion. Then I visited our daughter."

"She...she was fine?" She wiped away more tears.

"Yes, she was fine, and she *will* be fine."

"So you're saying whoever has taken our daughter won't harm her?"

"I don't know. I just know that we're not supposed to change the events of the past that affect the future. So I assume if we don't influence anything now, and we let things happen in their natural order, then our daughter should be alive and well until her future happens."

"Are you sure?"

Jael shook his head. "No, but that's the best we can do right now. We have to keep this information from Arete, Asana, and their people. I don't know if they have anything to do with our daughter, but if they want to harm us in any way, they might use her as leverage."

"What's her name?"

"Dinah Greenwoods."

More tears rolled down her face, and she wiped them off. "That's a nice name. She was nice, and so vicious the way she flies." She chuckled. "Just like you."

"That was when she flew with her weaponry wings. You should see her now. Magnificent with her real wings."

"Is she going to be an angel?"

"I doubt she would want that. Let's talk about that later. We should leave now."

"Where to?"

"I'm taking you back to the house of Gods."

"But you said you don't trust everyone in the house of Gods."

"I can protect everyone, all my subjects. But after what happened in the last few weeks, I know for sure that I cannot protect you. Until I put Asana and Arete into their places, I don't want you to be in danger. And the house of Gods is the safest place right now."

"Can I visit our daughter?"

"I think we should minimize interaction until things settle."

She nodded.

They heard a squeaking sound coming from their bracelets. They looked at them and saw a red dot flashing on a shiny square surface. The dot flashed. Flashed again. Next to it were the letters REC. The lights flashed a few more times and then went out. Nothing else happened after that.

"What was that?" she asked.

"It's quiet now. It should be okay. Let's go," said Jael.

Charmine frowned. She had seen those dots before but couldn't recall when it was. So she let the thought go.

CHAPTER 8

Madeline stepped down from the motorbike. She peeled off her helmet, giving it back to Ciaran. "I will never ever ride with you again, Ciaran."

Ciaran grinned. "Only my little brother is afraid of speed."

"That wasn't just speed—it was ridiculously insanely suicidal speed. I have no intention of dying today. We have children to take care of, Ciaran. And don't try to be cute. Even that signature grin of yours won't save you."

"I'm sorry, First Councillor."

"No, you're not. But I'll deal with that later. It's on the record." She slapped his shoulder lightly.

"My bad," he said and grinned again.

She tilted her chin at a charming white townhouse at the end of a street in a quiet suburban area just outside New York. "Nice place."

"Indeed. I've been here a couple of times. It's nicer inside," Ciaran said as he stepped down from the motorbike.

"You said Diane teaches aikido at home. This doesn't look like a martial arts studio."

Ciaran chuckled. "It's larger inside." He wrapped his arm around her shoulders, guiding her to the door.

Suddenly, a wave of buzzing noise hit her mind. This wasn't one of her usual psychic episodes. In fact, it felt as if something was sucking her brain out. The pain was sharp and sudden, and it made her gasp out loud. For a brief second, she felt empty. She glanced around, unsettled.

"Are you okay?"

"Huh?"

"You seem disoriented."

"I'm just a bit dizzy."

"Let's get you inside." Ciaran slid his arm around her waist to guide her toward the house. At the door, he pressed the doorbell. They waited. For a while, there was no movement inside.

"Are you sure she's home?"

"My chip suggests that she is."

"Your chip? You tagged her? Is there anyone you don't tag, Ciaran?"

"I don't tag strangers, or those I don't care about." He frowned and looked at his wrist unit. "The data suggests she's here right now." He tilted his head and looked inside the house via a gap in the window. "We've got to get in. Are you sensing anything unusual, Madeline?"

She shook her head.

He pulled out his cell phone and dialed. There was no response from Diana's phone. Ciaran tucked the phone away. Madeline knew he was agitated, and she wanted to help, so she opened her psychic mind and scanned around to see if she could get any signal at all. But nothing seemed to work. Her mind scanner bounced back empty.

She tried for a second time. The same results occurred.

Ciaran spun around and swung a kick at the door handle. The handle broke, and he pushed his way in. "I'm sorry, Diana. There's no gentle way to go about this. I don't know how to pick locks."

They walked into the wide corridor of a warm and welcoming home. Everything was quiet. Too quiet for Madeline's liking. The sofa in the living room stared blankly at them. A vase with fresh flowers was positioned in the middle of the coffee table. On top of the marble fireplace, there was a small framed picture of Diana, Jenny, Arik, and a man in his sixties.

She pointed at the man in the picture. "Is it Arik's father?"

Ciaran glanced at the picture. "Yes. But Diana hardly mentioned the man. Arik has never spoken about him. The only person warmed to him is Jenny."

They searched around the house, but they found nothing. Ciaran looked at his wrist unit again. "The signal for my chip is totally off now. I can't call Diana's phone anymore."

Madeline squinted her nose. "Perfume."

"What?"

"I can smell perfume."

"Yes, indeed. The scent is very subtle. Diana doesn't wear perfume. It's not her style."

Madeline nodded. "It smells expensive. She must have had a rich visitor."

"Let's go, Madeline."

"Where to?"

"The explosion site. Diana was on the phone with Arik, and then his father came on. Then there was the explosion. When I called him, he said the explosion was at his studio, and that Diana was fine.

I didn't put two and two together because my chip on Diana's phone didn't flag a red code. Now I can't call his number anymore."

They had been on the highway for ten minutes when Ciaran made a sudden U-turn. "She has to be in the house," he said and accelerated.

In no time, they were back in Diana's house again.

Ciaran walked back and forth. Then his eyes landed on a faint mark on the hallway wall. "That wasn't here before."

It looked as if someone had carried a hard object down the hall and scratched the wall with it. He followed the mark and rushed down to the studio. The rectangular room was surrounded by white walls covered with Japanese artwork. The decor was so elegant it was hard to believe this was a martial arts studio.

"You sense anything yet, Madeline?"

She shook her head. But she knew Ciaran believed there was something here. He wasn't psychic, but his natural instincts were strong. He traced his fingers along a wooden bar, and there, he found a lever. As soon as he pulled it, a panel in the wall slid open.

He rushed in.

Madeline felt death there, but not with her psychic mind. There was the tangible stench of blood.

They hurried down to a basement where they saw Diana lying face down in a pool of her own blood.

Ciaran threw himself to the floor, picking Diana's lifeless body up and clutching her in his arms. Madeline could see the pain in his eyes, and his shoulders shook with rage.

She didn't know much about the relationship between Diane, Arik, and Ciaran. But she had heard once that Ciaran considered Diana his second mother.

"She's still warm. It must have happened after we left."

"You're saying she was here the whole time, Ciaran?"

"Yes."

"Why didn't I sense anything?"

He put Diana down and looked at her. "You were distracted."

"By what?"

"I don't know. But I hope you'll tell me one day."

"Are you blaming me for this?"

"Why would you think that?"

"I don't know."

"Ciaran..." she approached him and held his shoulders. He shrugged out of her grip and pulled out his phone. "I'm calling LeBlanc security. We need people on this."

His eyes were as cold as steel, and she could see the terrifying pain he suffered deep down when people he cared for were harmed.

A sharp signal flashed through her mind. She gasped. "I've got a signal, Ciaran."

He turned, looked her in the eye, and waited.

"The last thing Diana thought before she died was *Arik, forgive them, son*."

He nodded and turned away.

"Ciaran, did you hear me?"

"Yes, she wanted Arik to forgive whoever killed her." He gazed into her eyes. "But she never asked me to forgive the cowards that shot at her back." He turned and walked out the door.

CHAPTER 9

Arete sauntered into the long, dark, and smoky corridor of the underworld dungeon to visit the minor god of the underworld he partnered with. He'd forgotten the god's name. Again. He had reminded himself to memorize it, but he forgot it every single time.

He looked around and found a quiet corner. Before the minor god entered the hall, Arete pulled out the tablet he had with him and did a quick search through his notes. There it was. Xecheron was the name of the underworld deity he was dealing with.

Xecheron preferred to be called a god, but Arete knew he was nowhere near that caliber. He had no rank, and he was the disgrace of all those with rank in the underworld. He was always seeking to move up the ladder. Arete knew Xecheron would never get anywhere, but his motivation served Arete's purpose well, so he went along on the ride with the power-hungry deity.

Xecheron. He muttered the name a couple of times in an attempt to memorize it.

The minor deity stepped into the hall, accompanied by an elaborate backdrop of smoke, light effects, and servants. Xecheron called it his "ceremonies." Arete rolled his eyes inwardly. If one had to resort to such elaborate methods to impress and to prove one's credentials, it definitely said something about one's character.

Xecheron settled on a thronelike chair, positioned at the top of a raised platform. Arete swallowed hard to avoid rolling his eyes again because if he kept doing that, his eyes might accidentally do it for real. He shuddered when he visualized that.

"What can I do for you?" Xecheron said in a trying-to-be-royal tone. "We just spoke."

"Using your magical talisman? Yes, we did talk. But I have something to show you now. It's called *technology*, and I don't think your talisman can handle it."

"All right, but be quick. I'm busy."

Arete nearly rolled his eyes, but he stopped himself. He switched on an electronic pad and played a record of the dialogue between Jael and Charmine.

Xecheron's jaw dropped. "Did you lock them inside that thing?"

"No, my dear god Xecheron. This is called a recording. In lay terms, I'd say we captured their voice. That's what this technology can give us. They didn't know my technology could hack into the device they were wearing. That technology is fifty years old—in Earth time, that is. So, although it does help them travel cross dimensions and worlds, it's vulnerable to hacking." Arete looked at Xecheron's face and sighed. "Xecheron, all I'm saying is that Jael and Charmine—the angel couple you're supposed to kill, remember?—they—"

"Yes, yes, I remember." Xecheron waved his hand in frustration. "The *technology* says that the angel couple has a daughter in the material world. And you think I can use the daughter as leverage to kill the parents, right?"

Although Arete didn't like the way Xecheron dragged out and put a sarcastic emphasis on the word technology, he had to admit that the god's mind wasn't as rotten as his looks.

"I would hope so. I just want to collaborate and make your job as easy as possible."

"Well, you know her name is Dinah, right? Wouldn't it be simpler to just kill her than to make a trip down here?"

"Oh no, it's not about me. It's about you, Xecheron. I have no use for Dinah's death. But you could use the daughter's death to make to the parents vulnerable. I know you're not scared of them, but they *are* angels. I know nothing about the angel business, but as far as I'm concerned, we want to gain as much advantage as possible."

Xecheron nodded.

Arete almost giggled from delight. Dinah had killed the giant, Roallix. There was no way in hell he would pick a direct fight with her. Not in a million years. He cleared his throat. "I know you are powerful, and your resources are unlimited. But you shouldn't have to spend much if you don't have to, right? Dinah is just an ordinary Iilos citizen. Her life isn't worth much to us. But it would cost the parents a great deal to know their daughter died in the hands of the mighty underworld god, wouldn't it? They're angels. They have their pride."

"Yes, yes, I hear you. There's no need for a long speech. I don't need an education from you about what I can and can't do."

"So what are you saying, Xecheron?"

"I'll consider this."

"There is no time to plan, Xecheron. You heard the recording. Please consider taking this opportunity. To get back to the house of Gods from the traveler's land, Jael and Charmine have to cross the transitional zone of the multiverse. You know that area. It belongs to no one. And thus, no one claims authority there, and no one will be responsible for any death or crime committed in that area."

"When will they be there?"

"Soon."

"All right. I'll get my fighters. I have to kill Dinah first and bring the news to her parents. Do you know where she is at the moment?"

"She's in Xiilok, and I know precisely where she'll be. But I have to warn you in advance—she's with Arik. The guy is supposed to handle the Amalgam world, so he is powerful."

"What's his talent?"

"I don't know. But I can help lure Dinah away from him. I have a few tricks up my sleeve."

"All right, let's hear them."

Xecheron gestured toward a stone table. Arete delightedly pulled out some equipment and approached the table for a serious discussion.

CHAPTER 10

As they walked into the lavish entrance of the LeBlanc New York headquarters, Madeline shuffled through her memories to find an occasion when Ciaran had mentioned Arik's family and found none. She had never heard of Arik before this trip, and every day that went by, she uncovered new things. She just wished she didn't have to learn new information via tragic events.

Ciaran had left an anonymous tip with the police about Diana. When he watched the news on his private screen as the police entered the house and discovered the body, she saw what she had never seen in him before—regret. He had lost so many people he cared about in several battles—some for good causes, and some just to defend himself and his people. But those he had lost had been prepared to fight with him and make sacrifices.

Diana was a trained fighter, yet she fought for peace and was an innocent bystander in the multiversal war.

Normally Madeline just used her psychic ability to poke around, but it dawned on her now that she might lose her talent. She wasn't sure what was happening, but after a few of the buzzing noise episodes, her mind seemed empty. There was no need, however, to alarm Ciaran now. Her psychic ability was the only reason he had brought her on this mission, so it would be best she kept quiet.

Adam Gardner, the current acting CEO, rushed in as soon as the steel door of the meeting room slid open. Ciaran sat at the end of the long meeting table. Madeline sat next to him. She knew Ciaran had arranged their seating positions for a reason. By the time Adam had walked from the door and around the long table to reach Ciaran for a handshake, Ciaran had already made a full evaluation of him—his ability, capability, and most importantly, whether he was trustworthy.

That was why Ciaran was lethal in his business—he was actively involved. When he let go, he missed things, and one of those things was Lindsay's betrayal. Ciaran could tolerate almost anything, but he had a very poor tolerance for betrayal.

"Mr. LeBlanc." Adam reached his hand out for a handshake.

"Ciaran."

"Yes, Ciaran. I am so sorry about Lindsay. I'll make all the necessary arrangements for his family…"

"So you haven't yet made the arrangements? When did they hear about his passing?"

"Two days ago. Look, I'm so sorry…but Lindsay didn't have plans for a successor, so there were a lot of details to handle when the accident happened."

"Indeed. I wouldn't think he planned for his death." Ciaran's eyes were as cold as steel, and he was wearing his signature unfathomable look. Adam had no way to tell what Ciaran was thinking, but Madeline knew her husband too well. She didn't need her psychic ability to help her. She knew Ciaran was trying to evaluate whether Lindsay had betrayed him or had been blackmailed by a force in the multiverse.

"When did you start, Adam?"

"Three days ago. And I'm qualified. I can show you—"

"No need to prove yourself to me. What have you done regarding Lindsay's family, apart from offering condolences and money?"

"That's all so far. But if you want us to do something more..."

"I'll need to use Lindsay's security team."

"We recruited a new team yesterday."

"Under whose order?"

"No one's, Ciaran. Lindsay's team dismissed themselves after hearing the news about his death. There was nothing we could do. We had to get a new team assembled yesterday."

"All right. Do you understand that Lindsay's team used to run several special ops for my family?"

"Of course. That's why they were a designated team. Because I didn't have exact information about what they did, I recruited them based on standard procedure."

Ciaran nodded. "I'll need their files and credentials in my computer system right away. And I'll need to see the team leader."

"Yes, Ciaran." Adam pulled out his electronic pad and typed in his commands. "The files are in your system now, and we got lucky—the team leader is on his way in right now." Adam looked toward the door as it slid open.

There, Madeline observed her crisis walk in as if in slow motion.

She hadn't foreseen this at all. Not only that, she was very sure that right now her psychic ability was dead. She couldn't even concentrate enough to consider whether it was a temporary loss or permanent.

"This is Jett," Adam said.

As Jett approached and shook Ciaran's hand, his eyes zeroed in on her.

"Jett who?" the words came out of her mouth before she could edit them.

He turned and looked at her. He still looked the same after all this time—exceptionally tall, masculine face, striking blue eyes, and a quirky smile. "Just Jett."

She looked at Ciaran and saw he had caught the connection. She wouldn't have expected less of him. "Ciaran, may I have a word with you?" she said and strode toward the door.

Outside the room, she turned and looked at him. "I dated him briefly in college. My first year. Just so you know." She cleared her throat and looked down.

Ciaran tilted her chin up and rubbed his thumb over the dimple on her left cheek. "You were young, and you dated a guy in college. That's hardly breaking news, Madeline. Why are you so worried?"

"Because I didn't tell you before."

"Everyone is entitled to their privacy."

"We agreed there would be no secrets between us, Ciaran. But we were young, and we committed a crime. He took the hit and went down for it. That was why I didn't tell you. It looks as if he has a new life now. So I'd appreciate you not looking into his past."

Ciaran's eyes grew intense for a brief second then returned to their normal unfathomable look. "Now that's something more than just an ordinary college date. And yes, I'll take your word that he is a new person now and we can trust he'll do the job he signed up for."

"Thank you." *Now that was stupid,* she thought. She had just thanked Ciaran for leaving her ex-boyfriend alone! But as much as she felt like an idiot right now, there wasn't anything she could do about it.

The fundamental rule of their marriage was that there would be no secrets between them. It wasn't that she hadn't honored their promise to each other for the most part, but she knew there was something she had not ironed out, even though she didn't really know what it was that she was withholding. She could see disaster coming her way like a train at full speed. She didn't know how to stop it or even jump out of the way.

CHAPTER 11

Madeline was totally uncomfortable about Jett escorting them to the site of Arik's father's house, but she guessed their time was limited, and Ciaran didn't have many options. Ciaran was meeting with Adam regarding some of the critical aspects of the LeBlanc business, which according to Ciaran had nothing to do with Eudaiz. She took the opportunity to take a walk down the street. She wanted to buy him a pair of beautiful leather gloves.

If dawned on her that they had never had a chance to be a normal couple. They had met due to unfortunate circumstances and hadn't even dated before they got married. And then there was this— there were always important calls they had to respond to, things that were a matter of life and death to humankind and all that.

Before she knew it, they'd had children and had ended up in space.

Well, it wasn't exactly that cut and dried. She shuddered thinking about how many times Ciaran had almost died in front of her—and vice versa. Their lives were stuffed with one mission after another. While Ciaran had always managed to sneak in a few little surprises here and there, she had actually never done anything for him as a girlfriend.

What could she possibly buy for a man who already had everything?

So she was pleased she had come up with the idea of gloves to cover his beautiful long-fingered hands that were always freezing because he never remembered gloves. He loved to handle computers and any technology and was quite hands on. He thought gloves on and gloves off would slow him down too much and would never buy them for himself.

"There you are!" she said and smiled at the boutique on the corner. She had frequently visited there when she worked as a journalist. Handmade clothing from a tailor was a concept she assumed had become extinct a long time ago. She didn't know how the tailor sustained his business, let alone—

"Oh Madeline!" the tailor exclaimed, interrupting her thoughts. "Long time no see! Look at you! You look like a princess."

She smiled at Bob, his hair now almost completely gray and his voice dripping with a heavy Italian accent. She hugged him. He had always treated her like a daughter. She was his princess.

"Don't tell me something happened to your red leather jacket!"

She had lost it in the fight through the Daimon Gate. It had been a life and death battle for her, and she was lucky to be alive. But all that didn't matter to Bob. All he knew was that the jacket he made for her hadn't survived.

Seeing the look on her face, he nodded. "All right, all right, my little princess. That is okay. I will make you another one."

"How are you, Bob?"

"Good. I am very good." He turned her around. "You've lost some weight."

She rolled her eyes inwardly. That just wasn't possible. She'd had two kids. And her home robot in

Eudaiz followed her every morning, threatening to scan her body and report her body mass index. She had never read the report, but she was quite sure weight loss wasn't a part of it.

"Let's make it black leather this time. I've just had one of the most beautiful leathers just imported from my homeland—"

"Bob?"

"Yes, dear?"

"I'm here not for me. I'd like to use that beautiful leather of yours to make a pair of gloves for my husband."

"Not a problem at all. He will be so pleased with the quality of the leather. Now, I might need some measurements... Wait, did you say husband?"

She grinned. "Yes, I did."

"Oh, my darling, congratulations! I am so happy for you!"

The doorbell sang lightly, and a customer pushed in. Bob paused and looked. Then a smile brightened his face. "Oh dear, I should have guessed. You were both so close. You're a perfect couple."

She turned around and saw Jett standing at the door.

"Excuse me," she said to Bob and rushed toward the door, pushing Jett outside.

"What are you doing here?" she asked.

"You're LeBlanc's lady now, but I didn't think you owned this shop."

"What we had was the past—"

"And a beautiful one it was."

She stared at him. "You don't blame me for what happened, do you?"

"No."

He held her shoulders. "I've never thought twice about that decision, but what I didn't expect was how much it pained me when I figured out I could never see you again. It was worse than death."

"You're a bigger man than that, Jett. You've rebuilt your life. You're now working for one of the largest conglomerates in the world."

He smiled. "Thank you for the reminder, Lady LeBlanc."

"I know the reality of it hurts you, but you'll have to deal with it, Jett. Not only am I married to Ciaran, I have a family and important matters to tend to."

"Understood. I'm not saying anything to try to intrude on your life. In fact, I didn't plan to see you again."

She nodded. "I told Ciaran about us."

"I was sure you would."

"You understand, right?"

"Sure."

She nodded. "So how are you? What's your new life like?"

"Well, since we haven't talked for such a long time, it's really not that new. I spent most of my time in Asia and have just recently moved back to the States."

"Where in Asia?"

"Not China, if that's what you're thinking." He grinned. "I operated my business mostly in Vietnam and Cambodia. And no, you can't ask me what kind of business. I'm finished with it, though, so I was on a break in New York. It's such a trick of fate. I heard the LeBlancs were looking for special security ops. I'd always wanted to work for them, so I jumped at the chance."

"You always wanted to work for the LeBlancs? But you were so laid-back back in the day."

He put on his brilliant smile again. "People change."

"Sure."

"How's Jo?"

She couldn't possibly tell him that Jo, their mutual best friend, was now Sciphil Four and managing a Eudaizian district of a multimillion citizens. She cleared her throat. "She's fine. Just got married and lives in another country. She works for the LeBlancs, too. You know...special ops. She wouldn't be able to reveal her location or contact you."

"I understand. She's married, huh?"

"Not only do people change, Jett, they move on!"

He nodded. "Understood." He gazed into her eyes and held the eye contact for so long it made her uncomfortable. "You haven't changed much."

"I have."

He reached his hand up and rubbed his thumb over the dimple on her left cheek. "That hasn't changed."

"Hey!" She pushed his hand away.

"Madeline!"

She turned around and saw Ciaran approaching. Her psychic ability wasn't working right now, and she really didn't think his unfathomable look would help at all, but it was all she had to go on at the moment.

She turned toward Jett and saw him smiling warmheartedly at her.

CHAPTER 12

Madeline walked by Ciaran's side, but it seemed like there were oceans between them. She couldn't read his mind, and he didn't give her anything to go on. They were entering a small but exclusive apartment where Lindsay's family lived. Jett and his security team had gone ahead to clear the area before they arrived.

Jett came back to the living area where Ciaran stood waiting. Ciaran had still not said anything. He would normally ask her if she could sense anything with her psychic ability. But it was off now, so she stood there feeling useless.

Adam entered the living area, looking as pale as a sheet.

Still, Ciaran said nothing.

"There's no sign of them. We haven't received a ransom note, but that might come later," Jett said.

"Lindsay was on private business in England for the LeBlancs. The next thing we know, he was dead in an accident, and his private security team walked. Now his widow and their daughter are missing. I don't think this has anything to do with official business," Adam said, looking straight into Ciaran's eyes.

It took guts to be CEO of the LeBlanc business, Madeline thought.

Ciaran nodded. "You're right, Adam. This is a private matter. So I suggest you go back to headquarters."

"I can send more people—"

"No, I'll contact you when I need you."

Adam nodded. "I'll leave the special ops here with you. Please feel free to use them for whatever you need."

Ciaran nodded. As soon as Adam left, he turned toward Jett. "Could you check around the outside of the building, please? See if there are any traces of them."

"I've already done that."

"You can never be too careful."

As soon as Jett exited the room, Ciaran pulled out his personal scanner and turned on his wrist unit. Madeline knew there was nothing Ciaran's Eudaizian technology would miss. The device flashed a blue light, and then data started to stream onto the screen. Ciaran frowned.

In a short moment, he looked at her and said, "There's nothing supernatural here. Before he died, Lindsay said they wanted the primer, and he wanted me to protect his family. But whoever captured his family wasn't supernatural."

"I always thought it was Arete, planning everything for the multiverse hologame he challenged us to," she said and tried to will her psychic ability to work again. Nothing happened.

"Let's go," Ciaran said and took her outside the room.

Back in front of the building, Ciaran got his motorbike ready. Jett and his team parked their cars right behind him. Ciaran pulled something out of his pocket and showed it to Madeline. It was a small jar, but she couldn't tell what was in it. When she approached to take a closer look, he slid it back into his pocket.

He grabbed his helmet. But when she reached for hers, he stopped her. "No, Madeline. You stay here with Jett." He looked at Jett. "Make sure she's safe."

"No—" she started, but before she could let out the second word, Ciaran had hopped on his motorbike and zoomed ahead. From the corner of her eye, she saw the white van that had followed them this morning go straight through the red light to give chase to Ciaran.

"That van stalked us this morning." She darted toward the car. "Come on, Jett."

Jett followed Madeline back to the car. "Ciaran said to stay here."

"He told *me* to stay, not you. So you're going to follow him. I'll just sit in the car."

Jett hesitated.

"Well, if you won't do it, I'll drive."

"Okay, fine." He got into the car and headed in the direction Ciaran had gone.

In the car, which she was sure was bulletproof, Madeline punched a button to roll the window down. She was amazed she guessed right. Normally she wouldn't even know which button to press. With her psychic ability gone, she would have to use her eyes and common sense to follow Ciaran.

"Don't do that, Madeline!" Jett yelled at her.

She pulled out her Eudaizian laser gun. "Watch me."

"Is that a stun gun?"

Jett had just referred to Eudaiz's most advanced weaponry technology as a stun gun! She shrugged and said, "Sort of."

"Well, you can't shoot anyone with a stun gun from inside a car, so I guess you can hang on to that gun if it makes you feel better. But don't brandish it openly. People will see you and call the cops."

"Fine." She lowered the gun.

Jet pushed a button to roll the window up. "If people shoot at us, I'm sure they won't be using stun guns. The windows are bulletproof. I promised Ciaran I would protect you."

"No, you didn't. He told you to do so because that's your job. But you signed up with the LeBlanc corporation, not with me. I can walk faster than you drive. If you don't speed up, I'm going to get out of the car and walk."

"I can't let you get out."

"Then drive faster."

Jett swallowed some profanity and accelerated.

"Why can't you call Ciaran and ask him what his plan is?"

"First, he's driving. I shouldn't distract him. Second, he won't tell me."

"He won't tell his wife what he's doing?"

Madeline glanced at Jett and saw a flash of genuine concern on his face. She said nothing. She couldn't possibly tell Jett that she and Ciaran were no longer normal humans and that they had been to numerous battles before in worse situations. At critical moments, Ciaran never communicated his plans over technological devices. He had learned a very expensive lesson on his way to the throne in Eudaiz.

In a short while, they were outside New York, where the roads were quieter. She asked Jett to close the distance. As soon as they turned into a quiet industrial area, she saw Ciaran stop his motorbike and wait. The lane curved a bit and was crowded with containers and barrels, so Ciaran couldn't see them from his vantage point.

The white van approached and stopped.

Ciaran walked toward it in the open field.

What if they shoot at him? She shuddered at the thought. Yes, they had eudqi—the most precious source of power in the Cosmo. But they had never had time to master it. The only thing she knew for sure was that if they had their eudqi on, they had superpowers, but at the same time, if they were hit at a critical point, it would be fatal. If they had their eudqi turned off, they would be just like humans, but their eudqi would heal almost all injuries.

Sometimes she thought that the decision of having the eudqi on or off depended on the chance of their winning a fight.

She didn't have her eudqi on because Ciaran had asked her to keep it off to avoid being tracked. She concentrated and turned her power on. She could feel the power rushing through her veins and triggering all her senses.

But she still couldn't find her psychic ability.

Eudqi and the Silver Blood were supposed to enhance natural talent, but for her now, turning the energy on only amplified her senses.

From the van, a group of four people stepped out. The elegant woman they had seen that morning in the passenger seat headed the group. The men walked behind her. Ciaran smiled at the woman, the smile he'd killed so many women with. And that was only counting those Madeline knew of.

One of the men trailing behind mumbled, "Are you sure that's the Eudaizian guy?"

"No, but I wouldn't let that much money slip away even if it meant shooting the wrong man." He discreetly pulled out a gun.

If Ciaran didn't have his eudqi on, there would be no way he could have heard their conversation.

She turned and could tell Jett was concerned. He wouldn't have been able to hear what the men said, but he could see even from this distance that a goon had pulled a gun and was standing where Ciaran couldn't see him.

CHAPTER 13

Jett pulled out his phone to call Ciaran, despite his inner voice telling him to do otherwise. His few years of training in the special forces should have served him better than this.

Madeline said, "Don't! It's too late, and it will only distract him." Then she charged out of her hiding position, running like the wind and leaving him behind, embarrassed.

He ground his teeth and ran after her.

When they closed the distance, Jett realized Ciaran still had not seen the gunman, but he did see

Madeline running toward him, brandishing her gun.

Come on! Jett thought. If Ciaran had any combat training at all, he wouldn't pull his gun out now because he would be slower than his opponents. He had to pretend he didn't see Madeline.

Ciaran did just that.

He ignored her and instead smiled at the woman in the group. Jett had to give it to him. How could a filthy rich guy, polished from head to toes, be so agile and seem sharp as hell in a critical combat situation?

"Stop!" Madeline yelled.

"Oh fuck," Jett cursed out loud as he knew the consequences of her action.

The group approaching Ciaran stopped and turned around, looking at her. When they turned their backs on him, Ciaran pulled out his gun.

He gunned down two men of the men in front, and the third one grabbed the woman and charged away. The two gunmen at the back turned and fired at Madeline. She shot back and gunned one down.

She was fast, but not fast enough. The last gunman already had a bullet leaving his gun muzzle and heading in her direction.

Once more, Jett had to act against his inner voice, which was cursing his stupidity right now. He pushed Madeline aside and copped the bullet for her.

He heard another shot and was certain Ciaran had put down the last man.

Jett was lying face down, feeling the impact of the bullet.

Madeline flipped him over. There, he saw tears in her eyes, the same tears she had shed years ago when he took the fall in a fatal college incident. He knew she was innocent, but all the evidence back then had pointed to the contrary.

"Jett!"

He groaned.

"What were you doing, you idiot?"

"I'm wearing a bulletproof vest." He winced and grabbed his shoulder. "It'll only be a bruise."

"You don't wear a vest on your head."

"I'd never stick my head out to stop a bullet. Not even for you, Madeline. So don't worry. You don't owe me anything."

Ciaran approached. "What are you doing here? I told you to keep her safe. You're fired."

Jett stood up. "Isn't that what I just did? I copped the bullet that was supposed to be yours. You're reckless, Ciaran."

"Excuse me?"

"I guess nobody has ever told you the truth because you pay them. Well, here's some breaking news for you. If you want to play it cool in front of those gangsters, then fine. That's your business. But you almost got your wife killed. I have no idea how she can run so fast and shoot with that stun gun of hers, but the bastard pulled his gun out. You would've taken that bullet if not for her yelling."

"You and she are not supposed to be here."

"You told her to stay. She didn't go after you. She got into the car and ordered me to go after you. If I didn't do it, she'd have driven herself. Do you think that would have been a safe option?"

"Do you think this is a joke, Jett?" Ciaran growled.

"That's enough, you two. Ciaran, if you have a plan, you have to tell me. You have a security team hired for you, so let's use their services."

"I don't need them to tail me."

"The tail just saved my ass, Ciaran."

"All right, let's just cool down. You didn't look like you had time to tell anyone your plans. But you do have time now, and if you trust me, tell me what you've got," said Jett.

Ciaran hesitated. Jett understood a man of Ciaran's caliber wouldn't trust just anyone.

"In front of the apartment," Jett said, "you flashed a small jar, and they chased you for that. You don't have to tell me what the jar is, but people will be back to get it. We need to prepare for that...your way, of course."

Ciaran nodded. "All right, here's plan B. Before he died, Lindsay said someone was after a jar of potion in his apartment. They took his family, and that means they didn't find the potion."

"You don't know what the potion is? The LeBlancs are in the pharmaceutical business after all," Jett said.

"Yes, but I no longer operate the business."

"Right. So what was the jar you had in front of the apartment?" Jett asked.

Ciaran continued, "Cologne that I took from the bathroom in the apartment."

"You've got to be kidding me," Jett muttered.

"Now what, Ciaran?" Madeline asked.

"We have to go see Arik's father. He didn't cooperate on the phone, so I have to talk to him in person."

"Who's Arik's father? What's his background? Are we getting in another fight? Because if we do, I'll need you both to wear bulletproof vests."

"No, we're good," Madeline said.

"You won't be when the bullet hits you."

"Okay, we'll put them on when we get there," Ciaran said and turned as if walking toward his motorbike.

"No, Ciaran, we're going in the car," Madeline said.

"All right," he muttered and walked toward the car. "I'll drive."

"Are you sure? It's a military-grade car—"

"Yes, Jett. I can drive anything with wheels and an engine."

"All right. I see you both have some sort of laser gun. I'd be happy to arrange real guns for you if you need them. Are you sure we won't be involved in another shootout?"

Ciaran chuckled. "No, we're more than happy with our primitive weapons. I'm not sure if there will be another fight, but if the situation goes awry, it's your top priority to keep Madeline safe, Jett."

"I'm not an invalid," said Madeline.

Jett smiled. "Even if I have to go against her will?"

Ciaran nodded. "Yes, even if you have to use force. I'd rather she be injured than dead."

"Hey!" Madeline protested, but Ciaran kissed her on the cheek to stop her words of protest.

"We want to finish this quickly and go home to the children, don't we?" Ciaran said.

Then in front Jett's astonished eyes, Madeline smiled and nodded to Ciaran as if she'd never protested before.

How did he do that? Jett asked himself as he followed Ciaran and Madeline to the car and sat like a meek dog in the backseat.

CHAPTER 14

Ciaran rushed through the broken front door into the open reception area of the art studio and ran down a corridor ruined by fire and explosion. The building seemed to have been evacuated.

His background check on Arik's father started to make sense. Quinn managed a large stage production company that regularly toured the world about thirty years ago. Their last tour to a highland city in Vietnam coincided with an explosion and fire at the Tri-Sun group.

Tri-Sun was a solar energy business and had nothing to do with the theater business. But Tri-Sun liquidated after the incident, and so did Quinn's company. Ciaran hadn't been sure about the connection before, but the more he thought about the timing of Quinn's renewed contact with his family after so many years of coldness and no communication, the more uneasy he became.

The two incidents had barely registered on any official Earth records. If Ciaran hadn't used his connection to the multiversal databank, he wouldn't have a bit of this information. What had been revealed was uncanny.

But he was afraid they were too late to fix anything. After all, what he did know had been illegally obtained from the database. He had to make sure he was on the right track before he stuck his neck out and did any further investigation.

He had underestimated the scale of this incident. He'd sent Arik and Dinah to the multiverse to deal with Xiilok because he thought it would be best for him to deal with Arete here. But this might be something totally different—something more Earthly than he thought. He was losing his advantage. His supernatural connections didn't seem to be of much help right now.

"This was a massive explosion!" Madeline said.

While that was blatantly obvious, he knew it was her way of letting him know, while Jett was in the room, that her psychic ability was still at rest, and she was getting nothing more than the ordinary visual.

Jett didn't seem to pay attention to what Madeline said. He looked around. "The authorities have been through this, and it was ruled an accidental gas explosion," Jett commented.

"Are you thinking there was perhaps another reason?" Madeline asked.

Jett nodded. "I have some expertise in my line of business. This looks like a gas explosion, but I'm sure it wasn't. As for the exact cause, I'll have to dig around a bit to be able to say."

"Then feel free to look around," Ciaran said.

"Who's that?" Jett shouted and darted to a corner of the room, where a panel of a wall moved. Ciaran followed, gun drawn, pushing Madeline behind him at the same time.

Jett kicked down the wall, and then they could see it wasn't a wall at all but a sliding door to an adjacent room.

In a corner of the room stood a man in his sixties. He raised his hands when he saw the trio enter, their guns aimed at him.

"Who are you?" Jett asked.

"Quinn," Ciaran muttered and lowered his gun. "Arik's father."

"Yes, that's me. You're Ciaran? We talked on the phone. How did you find me? The number doesn't register this address."

"I have my sources," Ciaran said.

"Perfume!" Madeline said.

"What?" Jett asked.

Madeline was right. Ciaran recognized the expensive scent they'd smelled at Diana's place.

"You shot Diana," Ciaran said and raised his gun.

"What? Shot? When? No...is she dead?" Quinn teared up and was obviously confused. He stepped sideways as if to get something.

"Stay still. Don't move, or I'll shoot you," Jett said.

"Is she dead?" Quinn asked.

"Yes, shot in the back. What kind of coward would do that?" Ciaran's eyes reddened.

"I just talked to her the other day," Quinn said.

"Who was the woman with you now?" Ciaran asked.

"I don't know what you're talking about."

"The same woman was at Diana's house. If it wasn't you, then that woman is the one who killed Diana."

"No, she wouldn't do that!"

"Oh, so you do know who I'm talking about. Who is she? If she didn't do it, she won't mind having a chat with me," Ciaran asked.

"Who are you, Ciaran, apart from being Arik's friend?"

"You don't need to know."

"I do, because if you are Arik's friend, and you don't have another agenda, it's not worth risking your life for this."

Ciaran's eyes darkened. "I'm a friend of your children, second son of your ex-wife. I know the family you long abandoned. Now if you don't tell me who the fuck that woman is, I'm going to dig the information out. There's nothing on this Earth that I can't find out."

Before Quinn could answer, they heard a crash upstairs.

"Jett, watch him. If he makes a move, shoot him. Madeline, please stay here and stand behind Jett," Ciaran said and ran up the stairs.

CHAPTER 15

The second floor of the building was dark and quiet. Ciaran scanned the area with his ordinary human eyes. He saw nothing unusual. He didn't have Madeline with him, and her psychic ability wasn't working anyway. His instincts told him to go back downstairs as he was at too much of a disadvantage in this darkness unless he switched on his eudqi.

The image of Diana dead in his arms washed over him like a tidal wave.

She had been the last advocate for peace, the last hope he hung on to. Whenever his wild, violent instinct hit him, he thought about her. That kept him calm and collected. It helped him think about the multiverse and the human race in a more positive light. The thought of her made him feel there was still hope for peaceful solutions in the Cosmos.

He had avoided making contact with her to keep her out of any trouble he faced. Now, that peaceful corner of his mind was destroyed. He could feel the rage coming back to him.

He switched on his eudqi.

The supernatural energy flowed through his system instantly. His senses were ultra-sensitive now, and he could hear a stream of uneven breathing behind one of the wall panels.

He approached with lightning speed and kicked down the panel. A shadow jumped toward him. Seeing the flash of a blade, he sidestepped, grabbed the attacker's knife hand, and twisted. He made a swift move and heard a grunt and the sound of the knife penetrating flesh. Warm blood spurted onto his hand.

A body flopped to the ground. He left it. He knew there were more people because the scent of perfume still hovered in the air, and even though he had just killed a man, he could still hear the ragged sound of breathing.

Then he heard scuffling and struggling sounds downstairs. He heard Madeline cry out, and Jett was shouting at someone, asking the opponent to drop his weapon. It sounded as if there was more than one male voice speaking at the same time, but none of them was Quinn's.

Listening to the sound downstairs was a mistake—a short moment of distraction his instincts would normally prevent. The next thing Ciaran knew, he took a kick to his abdomen and fell backward.

A large male stormed out from the darkness, following the kick by jumping and landing his knee in Ciaran's chest.

Normally, Ciaran would simply swivel and kick the man away. But his fatal eudqi point was on the left side of his chest. The man followed his knee with a punch. Ciaran had enough time to block it from hitting his fatal point, but the man's fist had still landed close to the spot.

He was dazed. It felt as if his chest was going to explode. He knew he couldn't take another punch.

In a blurred moment, with only a fraction of a second to think, he decided to take a gamble. He dropped his hands limply to the floor, pretending he had passed out from the pain.

It worked. The man stopped punching.

He picked Ciaran up by the collar and thrust him toward a wall panel. The panel slid open, and the woman he had seen in the white van and almost shot at that afternoon walked out.

Something in her eyes looked so familiar. But he was still too dazed to think clearly. Perhaps he hadn't needed to pretend to pass out—his body wanted to collapse to the floor right now.

He had underestimated the effect of having his eudqi on. He hadn't realized it was such as weak point, and it was a significant tradeoff. If he survived this, the first thing he would do when he got back to Eudaiz was make some type of protective gear to shield the fatal points of all those who had Silver Blood eudqi.

Even in the dark, the shape of the woman was exquisite and elegant. She was the epitome of beauty. She must have been incredibly beautiful when she was younger, because even now she was still overwhelmingly attractive.

"Who are you?" she asked as she slid her hand into his pocket and pulled out the jar. She glanced at it and then said with a strong French accent, "Cologne?"

"I believe so."

The man who was holding Ciaran raised his other hand in a fist and was about to punch him in the face.

The woman interrupted. "Don't hurt him. It's useless."

Ciaran tried to listen for anything going on downstairs but didn't hear anything.

The woman asked again, "Who are you?"

"And who are you?"

"I don't mean you any harm. I followed you because you called Quinn, and we tracked the signal. Then you went into the apartment where the jar of potion was kept."

"Which potion? Did you kill Lindsay's family? Did you kill Diana?"

"No, I didn't kill anyone. And I can't tell you about the potion."

"Then I can't tell you who I am."

"I can find out who you are. But I simply don't have time for that now. If you're a friend of Arik's, tell him bad people are coming for him."

"For what?"

"When the time comes, he will know."

Ciaran shrugged out of the man's grip and quickly felt the muzzle of a gun against his temple.

"I don't know who you are. But judging by the resources you can pull in a short period of time, I can tell you are a man of power. If you are Arik's friend, as Quinn said you are, tell Arik to think about what's at stake. Think about the bigger picture. If you want more information, it is downstairs."

The woman raised a hand and signaled. The man let go of Ciaran and pushed him away, sending him stumbling to the floor. The man and woman then vanished behind a wall panel. Ciaran scrambled up from the floor. He tried to work his way downstairs. Every step felt to him like moving a mountain. He didn't know how long this dazed effect was going to take to pass. He wanted to get downstairs quickly to see what was happening and to be sure Madeline was okay.

But his body wasn't cooperating. He would just have to take it one step at a time.

CHAPTER 16

The pungent stench of blood reached his nose before Ciaran hit the bottom step. He rushed down the remaining stairs and stormed into the room. In the far corner, Quinn's body and the bodies of two unknown men, riddled with bullet holes, lie crumpled on the floor.

In another corner of the room, Madeline sat on the floor with Jett.

He raced over. "Where were you hit?"

"The bullet just scraped my arm. Jett got one in the arm and one in the leg. Are you hurt, Ciaran? You don't look good."

"This isn't my blood."

"But you *are* hurt." She stared into his eyes.

He shook his head slightly, silently telling her not to ask. He didn't want to advertise in front of Jett the fact his body had been nearly paralyzed by the hit upstairs. "Try to rest your injury," he told her, looking into her eyes until she got the hint to turn on her eudqi to start his healing process.

She nodded.

"Can you hang for a bit, Jett? I'll take you to the hospital."

"Sure, I can wait. But there's no need for me to go to the hospital. I have my own people. They can patch me up."

Ciaran went over to the other corner to look at the bodies.

"They came out of nowhere," Madeline said.

He crouched next to Quinn and gently closed the man's eyes. Then he looked over at the bodies of the other men.

"Madeline, take a look at this."

She came over. When she stood next to him, he stood up, raised his gun, and pointed it at Jett.

Jett scrambled up and stood leaning against the wall.

"One wrong move and I'll savage your head, Jett."

"What are you doing, Ciaran?" Madeline asked.

"Who are you really, Jett?" He locked his eyes on Jett, making sure he didn't make any sudden movements. He disliked nasty surprises.

"I'm your security guy."

"Indeed, you were. And if you meant to kill me, I would have been dead. But I won't give you the chance to make that call again."

Madeline touched his elbow slightly. "What are you talking about, Ciaran? Two guys came out from behind the wall. I told them to put their guns down, but they didn't listen. They gave Quinn a gun as well. That made it three of them and two of us. Then they started shooting."

"Who fired first?

"That man." Madeline pointed at the man at the far corner. "He hit Jett's arm."

Ciaran smiled. "How lucky was that, Jett?

"Very."

"They had to open fire first to give you every reason to shoot in front of Madeline. Then she wouldn't suspect you. You wanted to keep her safe, so you bent down, pretending you were hurt, attracting the bullet to your leg and thus keeping it away from Madeline. In the meantime, you returned the shot, killing the man who opened fire. The kill shot was right in his temple. The next bullet was one to the head of the man who shot your leg. Those shots came too fast for them to react. Then the third shot was to your main target."

"That's a very good story," Jett said.

"That's speculation, Ciaran," Madeline said.

"The three kill shots happened so fast that they got hit but were still standing. You sprayed bullets everywhere to create chaos. If I check the laser marks from Madeline's gun, it'll show she barely hit anything. And if I check Quinn's gun, I'll find that he didn't fire a single shot."

"I don't know what you're talking about. The whole thing was pure chaos!" Jett exclaimed.

"I promised Madeline I wouldn't look into your past. But to clear yourself of this situation, I'll need to scan you." Ciaran flipped out a screen from his wrist unit.

"Scan me? Under what authority?"

"The authority that gives me the right to kill you right now, and nobody would miss you or even find a trace of you."

"Ciaran, you promised me," Madeline said.

"And I kept my promise. I didn't look into his past. But he *will* give me the scan." He held his wrist out. "It's a fast scan, and I promise it won't hurt—unless you have something to hide."

"What if I refuse to scan?"

"Then you'll have to take my bullet." He lifted his gun higher. "But unlike these dead guys, I won't miss."

"Ciaran, everyone has something to hide. This isn't fair," Madeline said.

"Diana never approved of violence. What did she do to deserve him shooting her in the back?"

"I didn't do it."

Ciaran continued, "If you don't want to scan, fine. Tell me who you're working for and what they want, and then I'll let you go."

"I work for you, don't I?"

"Don't try my temper!"

"Look, I—"

Ciaran shot Jett's already injured leg. "The next one won't be in your leg."

As Jett grunted from the hit, Madeline charged over, standing in front of him. "He might be hiding something, Ciaran," she said, "but he didn't kill Quinn in front of me as you suggest. I would like you to give him a chance to leave."

"Madeline, he can't just kill people without consequence!" Jett exclaimed.

"He can. Trust me, Jett. So if you have anything to say to save your life, say it now."

"I didn't do it."

"You heard him, Ciaran."

"I don't like pointing a gun at you, Madeline. Come over here with me."

"You think I'm going to take her hostage? I may not be noble, but I never shoot women in the back or use them as human shields. Madeline, please step aside."

"You don't know him, Jett. If I don't interfere, you *will* be dead."

"If he thinks he's God, let him kill me." Jett started to walk away.

Ciaran fired into the wall in front of him. "I said don't move. So if you didn't do it, tell me who did and I'll let you leave here alive."

Jett stared at him. "I don't sell people out."

He turned to leave, and Ciaran's finger strained at the trigger.

"No, Ciaran, I'm asking you to let him leave. Give him one chance. Please."

"No."

"I'm asking as your wife. I owe him my life. Twice."

"I am saying no as the top authority of Eudaiz. I'm asking you to consider your request as First Councillor, Madeline."

"This has nothing to do with Eudaiz."

"Yes, it does, and if he gives me the scan data, I'll prove it."

"Let him leave. My request stands. I'm asking as your First Councillor, too."

He lowered his gun. "As First Councillor, you do have that privilege, Madeline. Are you willing to use it on him?"

She looked at him, and a tear rolled down her face. She knew what he would say and do next.

"I have to take him out of here. If he leaves by himself, you're only one button away from finishing him."

"You know me well, Madeline."

She wiped the tears from her face and took Jett's uninjured arm to support him. "Let's go."

"If you walk out of here, Madeline, you are walking out on me, on our family, and on your official responsibilities."

"I'll take Jett to safety, and then I'll return to you, Ciaran."

"No, Madeline. You asked me to let him leave here alive, so I will. But if you walk out of here with him, that will be the end of everything."

"Ciaran!"

"I'll leave alone." Jett limped toward the door.

She looked at her husband. "He won't survive until tomorrow morning, will he?"

Ciaran saw the pain in her eyes and was sorry he had caused it. "I don't have an answer for you right now, Madeline."

She nodded, wiped her tears, and walked out the door.

PART TWO

CHAPTER 17

Ciaran slid down to the floor next to the dead bodies. His energy was leaving him in waves. He couldn't turn his supernatural power on to heal his body because he had been attacked close to his fatal point when he had his energy on. He'd have to heal himself naturally using his human power—which had been reduced to almost nothing.

His condition was deteriorating rapidly, and if he did nothing, he would soon be dead. For the first time in his life, he felt the powerlessness and hopelessness of being human.

But in this human form, he still had to follow through with the plan. People's lives depended on it. He adjusted some functions on his wrist unit, sending off the necessary commands. Then he disconnected with his networks.

He didn't want to get caught with the dead bodies, so he stood up and worked his way along the wall to exit the room. He saw the car parked outside. Madeline hadn't let Jett take it. But he didn't have enough energy to drive.

As the cold breeze blasted at his body, he zipped up his jacket and followed a dark alley, heading toward a light at the end. He glanced at his wrist unit, which was flashing an alarming red light, telling him about his deteriorating condition and warning him that he didn't have much longer before his body ceased to function. It was giving him a countdown.

Being Eudaizian sucked as well. The system treated creatures and bodies as inanimate objects— like cars. And eudqi was like gas. No gas, and the car stopped working. Ciaran felt the urge to chuckle but was too weak to do so.

The system clearly wasn't measuring his emotional energy, which at the moment was causing images of tomorrow's *New York Times'* headlines, reading "Mysterious billionaire Ciaran

LeBlanc found dead in dark alley" to flash through his mind. It would be a tragedy to his family, but to the computer system, it would be just another piece of data from Earth's news to be added to the databank of the multiverse.

New York's LeBlanc headquarters wasn't his turf. The new CEO was in no shape to help him handle any private business. London was a long flight away. He couldn't call Eudaiz central and ask them to send commanders to rescue him because he was more than sure his signal would be intercepted.

Arete and his allies were stronger than Ciaran had given them credit for.

And now, here on Earth, there may be new and unknown enemies. He didn't know which was worse—the known army of multiversal enemies or the unknown Earthly enemies.

He could call the Daimon Gate and other multiversal allies he had on his side—sticking with the enemies he knew would likely be the safer choice. But in his last moment of clarity, Ciaran chose to remain human and not engage supernatural forces.

Just before his leg started to give out on him, he saw the subway and the flashing lights of the oncoming train. He didn't know how he got onto the platform and onto the train, but the next thing he knew, he was flopping down on a bench on the train.

He closed his eyes briefly. Then he opened them suddenly.

Did I pass out?

He didn't know how long it had been since he first sat down and closed his eyes. He had no idea where the train was going, but he knew he shouldn't be there. He got off the train at the next stop.

He reeled along the railway terminal and out into a dark tunnel. He wouldn't last much longer. He didn't know where he was going or what he was doing. He needed help. That much he knew.

His knees buckled, and his legs gave up. He collapsed next to a dumpster. Before he closed his eyes, he could see the flashing light of another train coming.

As the train's movement made the tunnel shudder, his mind started to drift. He shook his head, waking himself up, and turned on his wrist unit. Ignoring the flashing red alarm about his condition, he coded a rescue signal, sending it to his friend, Dinah.

Then he peeled his wrist unit off and shoved it into his pocket. He couldn't afford to lose it if he got mugged.

Sitting on the ground, leaning against a dirty wall next to the dumpster, he stared at the tunnel. It looked so familiar. His mind started drifting away. An image flashed in his head. He remembered now.

Seven years ago, while he was mourning Juliette's death, he wandered into this tunnel and ended up saving the life of a little boy. For reasons unbeknownst to him, his subconscious mind had dragged him back here.

He saw the shadows of two people walking toward him from the darker end of the tunnel. He had been afraid of this, and now here it was. Every movement he made was painful and cumbersome, so he sat still and waited.

The two men stepped into the dim light of the tunnel. They said something he couldn't hear, but he figured they were asking for money. If they reached into his pocket, they would find the wrist unit that carried the top secrets of Eudaiz. He couldn't afford for that to happen.

One man grabbed him and started pulling him up from the ground. Taking advantage of the upward momentum, Ciaran pulled his gun and shot the man. As the man in front of him fell to the ground, the second man kicked the gun from his hand. It dropped to the ground and spun away, out of reach.

Ciaran couldn't stand up much longer, but he tried to remain as upright as possible. The second man was about to lunge at him. He knew the man wouldn't go for the gun because in doing so, he would have to turn his back on Ciaran, and he had no idea what other weapon Ciaran might have apart from that gun.

From the end of the tunnel, a male voice shouted, "Stop!"

The attacker froze and looked in the direction of the voice. A shadow darted toward them. Ciaran saw his attacker pull a knife.

Unsure whether the person who was trying to help him was aware of that, Ciaran shouted, "He has a knife!"

The attacker kicked Ciaran, sending him backward to the ground, as the shadow of his savior charged over and tackled the man.

Ciaran crawled toward the gun as the sounds of fighting and struggling echoed behind him.

Then someone grabbed his shoulder. He rolled over on the ground and swung his gun upward.

"No, no, don't shoot, Ciaran!"

In front of Ciaran was a familiar face. "Who are you?"

"Michael Fraser."

His mind started to drift again. He closed his eyes, and his arms seemed to weigh a ton. He dropped them to the ground.

"Come on, man, it's me. We have to get out of here."

Someone shook his shoulders. He remembered that name now. Michael Fraser—the boy he had saved seven years ago. He muttered, "What are you doing here? Aren't you supposed to be in school?"

"Lindsay had been checking in on me every week. But last week he didn't. He's never missed a check-in. I knew something's had to be wrong with him—and maybe with you. I didn't know what to do, so I came here. Come on, these guys are dead. We gotta go."

"You've been keeping tabs on me?"

"Not exactly...I just wanted to make sure you didn't cut off my living allowance. Oh come on, open your eyes. You gotta walk. I ain't going to carry you!"

"I misunderstood Lindsay." He was so tired. Michael said something else, but he couldn't hear anymore.

Darkness.

CHAPTER 18

Dinah descended to the dark alley and released Arik from her wings.

"This is the one and only time I rely on your wings to travel via the multiverse teleport, Dinah."

She smiled. "You might change your mind if you have to choose between me and the public transport. But Ciaran's in trouble. Using the official system isn't a good idea."

"How do you know it was him? It was an anonymous SOS message."

She gazed into the distance and muttered, "Not only it was him, but he was indeed in trouble."

In the dark alleyway in front of her was a young human boy, as beautiful as a vampire she had once seen on one of those screens in Xiilok—well, they were beautiful *before* they became Xiilok zombies.

The young man crouched next to someone who lay on the ground. The private wrist unit that Ciaran had given her buzzed like a machine gun on automatic discharge. Judging by the map on her screen, the body on the ground was Ciaran.

"Hey!" she shouted and spread her wings, flying toward the man. "It's too dark, Arik."

He ran on the ground, racing after her, his body glowing like a giant electric candle.

The young man, startled, fell backward and raised his hands as if in surrender. "Hey, I didn't do anything. He just passed out. The others had already beat him up when I got here. I just want to help."

"Who are you?" Arik asked.

"Michael."

"Ciaran!" Dinah checked Ciaran's pulse. It was weak. "He's totally out of it."

Arik grabbed the young man.

"Come on, let go of me, man. I just want to help Ciaran."

"How do you know his name? You take his wallet?"

Dinah opened Ciaran's shirt. That was always the first thing Madeline did when Ciaran was out. A large black and purple bruise spread across his chest. Madeline had never told her anything, but she guessed Ciaran had some sort of critical point on his chest.

From what she knew about Eudaizians, they operated on energy sourced from the tower. Ciaran's critical point must be on his chest. If he had been attacked there, it would cut off his energy.

He had probably underestimated the damage it could cause and thus hadn't protected it properly. She shook her head. He had learned a big lesson.

She pulled out her stack of needles and searched for the correct one. From behind her, the young human was still trying to convince Arik that he was on their side. She knew he was, but she didn't have time to help him now.

"There." She tapped her finger lightly on Ciaran's jugular where she had just given him a little boost to his system. When he was conscious, he would be able to instruct her as to what she should do.

Soon he stirred and opened his eyes. "Dinah!"

"There you are! Tell me what to do, Ciaran."

"I like your hair."

"You don't have to be polite. It turned white after a fight in Xiilok, and I chopped it short with a hunting knife. Ciaran, I gave you an energy boost, but it won't last long. Your energy level is alarmingly low."

He smiled at her. She didn't know how he managed that, but he always did. If she had the emotional capability of a human, she would fall for it. "I can sleep it off."

"Sleep? Do you mean the condition of body and mind in which the nervous system is inactive and consciousness practically suspended? Is that what you've been doing?"

He chuckled. "Not intentionally. When I first came to Eudaiz, it happened every twenty-four hours if my supernatural power decided not to help. That's what it's doing now—refusing to operate my body."

She helped Ciaran sit up.

"See, he's up. You ask him. See if I hurt him or not," Michael said.

"Ciaran, is this brat your son? He killed two guys here!" Arik exclaimed.

"He isn't my son, and he isn't a brat."

Michael raced over. "Are you okay? You scared the hell out of me."

Ciaran stood up. "You've grown up, Michael." He glanced over at the bodies. "I killed them."

"That's not the story Michael here gave me," Arik said.

"They wanted to rob me. I couldn't let them get the wrist unit. So I shot one, and Michael handled the other one."

"It was self-defense. He had a knife. I didn't have a weapon."

"You attacked him when he had a knife, and you had nothing?" Ciaran raised his voice.

"You did the exact same thing before. Otherwise, I'd have gotten my throat cut, Ciaran."

"That was seven years ago..."

Michael stared at Ciaran. "Seven years, two months, and twenty days."

Ciaran lowered his voice. "I meant I attacked a man with a weapon because I knew I could take him down. I'm a trained—"

"I am a Shotokan karate black belt ninth dan."

Arik approached. "Hmmm...so you're licensed to kill. As far as I know, the ninth dan black belt takes years to achieve. How old are you?"

"Fifteen." Michael still locked eyes with Ciaran. "But I was prepared to get my throat cut when I was eight. And someone told me life is worth living, and I can make a difference if I get an education and if I try."

"Which part of that isn't right?" Ciaran asked.

"I tried. But I need more than the money you throw at me. Every month, Lindsay gave me a different excuse. 'Oh, Ciaran is busy—he's in London for a very important meeting. Oh, Ciaran is in Asia this month. Oh yeah, he's in New York now, but will be in locked-down meetings all week.'"

"Michael, it might be hard for you to hear, but apart from money, there is nothing else I can guarantee you. The world isn't about you. I have more important matters to tend to, and people's lives depend on it."

"Right, so you're saving the world now!"

"Yes, literally. I refer to your world as Earth," Dinah said.

Michael laughed. "She's funny." Then he looked at Dinah's face. "You're serious! 'Cause I saw you flying with the wings, and he glowed like a candle. So...you guys are aliens? It wasn't a trick?"

Arik rolled his eyes.

Ciaran reeled and leaned against the wall. "I need a place to crash right now."

"What does that mean?" Dinah asked.

"He needs a bed, a hotel. And off the record so we stay under the radar," Arik said.

"I can use my credit card. It's backed by LeBlanc Pharmaceuticals, so it's unlimited funds. And Lindsay told me my association with the LeBlancs won't be on record."

"That should do," Arik said.

Michael approached to help Ciaran walk. Ciaran shrugged him away and strode ahead. Then he leaned against Dinah's shoulder. Michael turned and looked at Arik, questioning.

Arik approached him and said, "Can you call the cops and leave information about these dead bodies?"

"Already done. Anonymous tip." Michael waved his cell phone then shoved it into his pocket.

"Thanks. Just so you know, Ciaran isn't mad at you. But Lindsay is dead, and he feels responsible for it. Kind of like the way he feels responsible for the world and humankind. If you take him as your spiritual father, you're in for a hard life. But for now, try to limit discussion of Lindsay in your conversation. That'll help a great deal."

CHAPTER 19

Madeline sat on a bench beside the sidewalk, waiting for Jett to come out of his friend's small medical clinic. After they left Ciaran, Jett had called his associates, and a car picked them up and drove them here.

She didn't know this part of New York at all. It was like a different country to her. She wondered how Ciaran was doing and whether he had taken the car she left for him.

Although her psychic ability wasn't working, she could still feel every vein in her body nearly bursting with anxiety. She promised herself she would hold tight until Jett had patched up his injuries and left for safety. Then she'd call Ciaran. He'd understand. It wasn't like they'd never had a fight before.

After a short while, she gave in to her anxiety and called Ciaran's wrist unit. A red flag and a text appeared on the screen: "You no longer have a connection with this unit."

Her head started to spin. She couldn't breathe.

"Madeline!" Jett's face loomed over hers. "Are you okay?"

"I... I can't..." She couldn't find the words. Tears started to fall, and her body began to shake.

The screen of the wrist unit stared at her, the red text glaring harshly at her.

Jett saw the text and muttered some profanity.

She shuffled through her contact list, but every number she tried to call came back with no connection. The screen of the wrist unit—her only connection with Ciaran, with Eudaiz, and her children—was as blank as her soul at that moment.

She looked at Jett. "I...I don't understand. I told him I'd come back."

"I'm sorry, Madeline." Jett pulled her into his arms and let her cry.

"I want to go home. I need to go home."

"I'll take you. Tell me where."

She stared at him. "I don't know." She started walking aimlessly. Jett grabbed her elbow and pulled her back.

"Madeline, you're scaring me. You're stronger than this."

"That was when I had nothing to lose, Jett. Now I have a family I treasure. People to take care of. If Ciaran doesn't want me anymore, I want my children." She pushed him away and kept walking.

"Where are you going?"

"To LeBlanc headquarters. I don't believe they don't have his number. If he wants to divorce me over this, I at least want access to my children."

"Let me take you."

She kept walking.

"Please."

She stopped and nodded.

"Before we head back to LeBlanc headquarters, I want to let you know one thing," he said.

"What?"

"Ciaran was right. I killed Quinn."

"I don't understand."

"Quinn was my target."

"Target?"

"I'm a hit man. Ciaran gave a correct account of what I did."

She walked back and forth, trying to digest the information. "Did you kill Diana?"

"No. I told you I don't shoot in the back. But my associate did. And I didn't lie about that. I didn't kill Diana. She was collateral damage."

"Collateral damage?"

"I'm an assassin, Madeline. I kill for a living. The fact that your husband knew precisely what I did suggests that he's killed before."

She slapped him across the face. "Ciaran has never killed for a living. What he does is fundamentally different from what you do."

Jett rubbed at his face. "I told you I'm not noble. I don't do anything for the greater good. But I care about you. This is bigger than you think, and I don't want you to get tangled up in the middle of it. You are my selfish little problem."

"Is Ciaran on your hit list?"

"No. If he was, he would have been dead by now."

"Did you plan all this? Our reunion? The incident in the house?"

"No, I just got lucky."

"I know your hit list must be long and extensive, and you won't give me any specifics, but is there anyone on it I need to worry about?"

"They just cut you out of their lives, didn't they?"

"Jett!"

"All right, I'm sorry. No. No one you should be concerned about, and even if there was, there's nothing you can do about it. I told you...this is a lot bigger than you think."

"I have to talk to Ciaran." She strode ahead.

"You don't have a car. Let me take you."

"All right."

A short while later, they parked across the street from the back entrance of a building three blocks away from the LeBlanc's New York headquarters.

"How did you know the CEO parked his car here?"

"I know his routines. Part of the job I signed up for." Jett chuckled. "But he's not on my list, so don't worry."

A man-shaped shadow approached the car park. It was Adam, the new CEO of LeBlanc Pharmaceuticals New York. Madeline approached him.

"Adam."

He turned around. "Oh, there you are. I was a bit concerned because your number was disconnected. I didn't know how to contact you. Don't worry—I got the message. Everything has been arranged for you."

"What are you talking about?"

"Your belongings in the hotel. There's not much there. Your previous apartment has always been listed with the LeBlanc's private properties. They've just released it back to you."

He gave her a large envelope.

"The keys and everything else are inside. Also, there are some temporary credit cards and some financial arrangements you can change later. Ciaran wanted to make sure you're comfortable."

"Did you talk to him?"

"No, I just got the memo from the executive secretary."

"Do you have his number?"

"No, he contacts us when he needs to. You know how he operates."

She was so numb she didn't know what to say. Adam nodded a goodbye and scurried away.

She opened the yellow envelope and pulled out a memo of instructions for arrangements to be made for Madeline Roux—her maiden name and not even her Eudaizian origin name. It was the human name she had used before she met Ciaran.

She felt Jett's hand on her shoulder. "Is everything okay?"

She turned and looked at him, but no words came out of her mouth. Then she turned around, darted toward a corner of the car park, and was violently sick.

CHAPTER 20

Arik, Dinah, and Michael stared at Ciaran over a coffee table in the sitting area of the hotel suite.

"You disassociated with Madeline! I thought you two were inseparable," Dinah said.

"On Earth, we call it a divorce, Dinah," Arik said.

Ciaran stood. "All right, so I've explained to you why Madeline isn't here. We have work to do. I have some suggestions regarding the primer for Dinah. I need to talk to you about your family, Arik. And I need to send Michael back to school."

"But I saved your ass last night!" Michael exclaimed.

"And I would like you to do it again in the future, so I need you to get more training and grow up a bit more. Then we'll talk."

"That's just bullying!"

"Yes, that's unreasonable," Arik said.

The lights flickered, and a wave of electronic static rushed through the room.

"Something's coming. Don't interact with it. Stand next to me, Michael."

"Okay, got it!"

A hologram-like image of a man and woman flickered several times then solidified. Standing in the middle of the room was the magnificent couple, Jael and Charmine. They looked at Dinah and smiled at her. The light around them dimmed gradually, and the halo softened. Soon they stood among others in the same space.

"Wow!" Michael gasped and then snapped his mouth shut when he felt Ciaran's hand squeezing his shoulder.

"Mother!" Dinah said softly, a tear rolling down her cheek.

Jael nodded. His angelic eyes softened. "I was taking her back to the House of Gods, but she insisted on seeing you before she entered the magical realm again."

"Don't interact yet, everyone. Wait until everything is settled," Ciaran said.

Everyone stayed where they were.

"How did you find me?" Dinah asked.

"Your mother is a traveler of the multiverse. She can sense and track things that I still don't understand," Jael said.

"She's a multiversal gypsy! Is that a word?" Michael gasped and got another stare from Ciaran, so he withdrew.

Ciaran spoke gently, but Dinah could feel the strain in his voice. "You're from the past and another mind dimension. I take it you had assistance crossing multiple time and space dimensions to get here."

Charmine smiled. "Yes, Sciphil Three of Eudaiz, the one you met at the fight on the hilltop, gave us the bracelets that help us travel."

She raised the arm with her bracelet and pointed at Jael's with her other hand.

"Why are they flashing red?" Arik asked.

"They've been doing that for a while, making noise and flashing. But nothing has come of it, so we figured that was just how they worked," Jael said.

"Are they time bombs?" Michael asked.

"I don't know what that is, young man." Jael smiled again.

"Can they take the bracelets off?" Arik asked.

"No, those are dimensional transformation resistance bands. I recognize them. It's Iilos technology," Dinah said.

Ciaran spoke softly, "Once they start using the bracelets, they cannot take them off, or they'll die."

"We're aware of that," Charmine said. "I don't know what a bomb is, but judging by the look on this young man's face, it must be something lethal."

"His name is Michael. And yes, bombs are lethal," Arik said.

"Why would Sciphil Three want us dead?" Charmine asked.

"It might not be a bomb. Could you tilt the screens toward me so I can take a look at the signal?" Ciaran asked.

Jael and Charmine did as he asked.

Ciaran studied the screens then turned around, looking at the group. Everyone saw the word REC on both of their screens, meaning their dialogue was being recorded.

The devices the angels were wearing had been hacked.

Ciaran signaled everyone to remain silent and said, "That's quite normal."

He turned his unit on and typed in commands. He nodded at Dinah. She did the same. A beam of blue light strobed from Ciaran's wrist unit to Dinah's then bounced to Jael's and Charmine's.

Ciaran said, "They're jammed. We've got five seconds. Jael and Charmine, Dinah will take you back to your dimension. I'll insert an alternative program into your device so it thinks it's listening but it's not. Tell Dinah what has happened since the bracelet started beeping. She'll adjust the program accordingly and keep me posted. Understood?"

Everyone nodded. Ciaran looked at Dinah, and they both switched off the blue light. Ciaran entered new commands into his unit.

Dinah turned around as Arik embraced her. He kissed her cheek, then her lips, and then let go.

Ciaran sent off another set of commands. Then he embraced Dinah, kissed her cheek lightly, and brought her to where Jael and Charmine were standing. Ciaran issued a three-dimensional print of a bracelet from his wrist unit and gave it to Dinah.

She looked at him then turned and looked at Arik. Smiling, she snapped the bracelet on.

Together, the trio vanished into another dimension.

Arik flopped down on a chair with his head in his hands.

Ciaran approached him and handed him another bracelet he had just created.

"What are my options?" Arik asked.

"If you love her, you have one option—wear the bracelet. The bracelet locks your profile of time and space with hers, so you'll be the same regardless of how long it takes for you to see each other again. But as you can see in the case of Jael and Charmine, it's permanent."

Arik took the bracelet, looked at it, and then snapped it on.

"I'll take Michael back to his place. Then we need to talk about your family, Arik. It's not good news." Ciaran and Arik turned and looked at Michael.

"He doesn't look like he's going anywhere even if you get a bulldozer in here. So whatever you need to tell me, let's hear it. It can't be worse than the fact that I lost my sister in Xiilok and Cooper lost his arm in an attack."

"What?"

"It's a long story. But I saved my Yellow Shield tribe. During the fight, Cooper and Jenny dropped to the side of the mountain. The next thing we knew, Cooper ran back to us, one arm missing, and said that Jenny had been taken by something manmade. Then he left during the night."

"So both of them are alive?"

"In theory. Cooper left a note, and Dinah suspected we would find Jenny and Cooper at the Red Shield camp. But we hadn't yet gotten there when she got your SOS message. So I don't know what to tell my parents about Jenny. All right, I've said my part. What did you want to tell me?"

CHAPTER 21

Dinah signaled so that Jael and Charmine stayed behind her. A short distance ahead was a stone cave wrapped by two gigantic stone angel wings.

"Why would someone want to live in a place like that?" Dinah asked.

"Asana always wanted to be an angel," Jael said. "When we jumped the light hundreds of years ago, he pushed me through the light because he thought I had the best chance to become one."

"That was *his* version of the story," Charmine said. "My version was that he wasn't good enough to be an angel. Or he wasn't game enough to jump the light, so he pushed you through."

Dinah chuckled and said nothing.

Jael continued, "He used to be a good man. But he was blinded by power and poisoned by Arete."

"I would call that greed, Father." The sound of the word *father* rolling off her tongue was strange, but she liked it.

"If it wasn't for that greed, I wouldn't have met your mother."

She smiled. "All right, I promise I won't hurt him for no reason."

"He's famous for his medicine and poison, Dinah. Be careful," Charmine said.

Dinah frowned. "Does he only handle potions, medicines, magic, and sorcery, or does he deal with technology as well? I mean, things like machinery and computer technology?"

Jael shook his head. "I know what you mean by technology. No, I don't think Asana is capable, nor does he have access to technology. But Arete does."

"So that means it couldn't be Asana who was spying on us. Arete manipulates the multiversal hologame and challenges every authority in the Cosmos. It has to be him."

Jael was worried. "Is he listening now?"

"No, he's listening to what we want him to hear. Ciaran planted a program, and I just added an adjustment to it." Then she turned around, looking at Jael. "Does this have something to do with aperture jumpers?"

"I'm not sure. But I know it has something to do with the connection of worlds. I was told something significant will happen in multiple worlds soon. But I don't know what it is."

"Do you know when?" Charmine asked.

Jael shook his head.

"If Asana had been an ally of Arete for a long time, do you think he'd know?" Dinah asked.

Jael nodded.

"So let's go and ask him to make our trip worthwhile," Dinah said.

Jael kicked in the door and entered, followed by Charmine and Dinah.

Asana was immersed in his medicine and cooking, paying no attention to the outside of his residence. He almost fell off his chair with surprise when the trio walked in.

"Jael, what do you want?"

"Asana, I see you've changed," said Jael.

"People change."

Jael chuckled. "I meant your eyes."

"If not for the prick Cooper and his girl, I wouldn't have ended up at the bottom of the well to eat worms—and have to live with these eyes."

"Cooper who?" Dinah asked.

"I think his last name is Donovan."

Dinah flew over and pounded on the man. "You don't *think*. His name *is* Cooper Donovan. And he's my best friend. What did you do to him so that he had to kick you down a well?"

Asana fell to the floor and raised his hand, seeking a truce.

Dinah wouldn't stop hitting him, and Jael had to drag her away. "That's enough, Dinah."

"What did you give Cooper that made him weak and allowed him to be captured?" Dinah shouted at him.

"I didn't do it. It was Arete."

"Arete? He's strong, but Cooper is a lot stronger. What did you give Cooper?" she roared. "He's lost an arm. Let me cut out your arm so you can see what that feels like." She grabbed a knife from a nearby table.

Asana cried out in fear at Dinah's tenacity. "I gave him wolfsbane because I wanted an exchange for the Daimon Gate privilege."

"You poinsoned him with wolfsbane?" Dinah asked.

"It's a hallucinogenic agent."

"I know what it is. But you wanted a Daimon Gate privilege. What do you have planned with Arete that's so big you need an escape hatch?"

"I...I..."

She kicked a pot of boiling water over. It poured onto a jar of potion and a basket of powder. Chemicals sizzled and bubbled. "Tell me!" she shouted at Asana.

"The triple aperture. That's what it is. Every five hundred years, the triple aperture combines the material world, the magical world, and the amalgam world. Whoever jumps the triple aperture will have ultimate power."

"The power of god, of course."

"Do you believe in that?" Jael asked.

"I do. But I don't trust Arete. The plan is for us to approach from three different worlds and jump together. But I know Arete will prevent us from jumping so he can get it all for himself. That's why I need a new plan."

"So who arranged for the humans to capture Cooper?"

"Arete, of course. He thinks we're stupid. He knows exactly where and when it will happen on Earth, but he'll never tell us. He handles the material world. The other two worlds will never have a chance to get close to the location."

"Where on Earth exactly?" Dinah asked.

"If I knew, I'd be halfway there already." Dinah nodded, and as Asana turned around, she jabbed a needle into his neck.

***

In a dark dungeon covered by rusty computer mainframe, Arete was working on his commands. The spying device he had planted underneath Asana's medicine table started broadcasting Asana's voice, saying, "He thinks we're stupid. He knows exactly where and when it will happen on Earth, but he'll never tell us. He handles the material world. The other two worlds will never have a chance to get close to the location."

Then there was the sound of chaos and struggle. And the sound of Asana drawing in his last breath echoed in the air.

"My condolences," Arete talked to himself.

CHAPTER 22

Jett put the food he had picked up at the nearby market on the table. His apartment was the safest place he could think of for Madeline to stay. But it was a rental he had for only a week. His life was adrift. He was used to it, though, and was quite content with what he did.

But the sight of her living in his apartment triggered all the memories and the dreams they had shared. He hadn't revisited those feelings in a long time. His line of work had never given him the luxury. He needed a long-term solution for this.

Madeline still lay on the sofa, staring at the wall as if he didn't exist. He offered the bed, but she wouldn't take it.

He crouched next to her on the sofa. "You can't do this to yourself, Madeline. You have to eat. You have to get up. I know it's hard, but that's life. If there's anything I can do to take back what had happened and fix it, I'll do it."

He brushed a strand of stray hair off her forehead. She didn't even bother pushing his hand away like she had before.

"Was anything between us real?" she asked.

"You mean what we had in college?"

She nodded.

"I told you that was the only real thing I've had in life. We were happy, remember?" He sat down on the carpet and leaned against the coffee table.

"Yes, indeed, we were very happy."

"Freyja," he said.

"You remember that?" A tear rolled down her face.

"Of course I do. If we had a daughter, we'd call her Freyja."

She laughed a little as another tear rolled down her face.

"What are your children's names?"

"Caedmon and Lyla."

He nodded. "They must be beautiful."

"Yes, they are. And way too smart for my liking."

"Ciaran will change his mind. You'll see them again. It's your right, Madeline."

She shook her head and wiped away another tear.

Jett grabbed his pack from the table, pulled out a cigarette, lit it, and took a drag.

"We haven't been married for long, but we know each other well. There have been countless times I pulled things off, but I don't think I can do it this time. I made a mistake." She started to cry.

"It's my fault. Come on." He squashed out his cigarette and pulled her into his arms. "I'm sorry. Is there anything I can do?"

She shook her head, and the tears continued to fall. He didn't know what to do, so he just held her in his arms and rocked her. She cried for a while then fell asleep.

He tucked a blanket around her and went outside. He called his contact. "I want out."

A staticky filtered robotic voice answered him, "You have to at least finish the first part of our agreement."

"I'll give you back the money."

"It's too late for that. I can't find a replacement quickly enough. We can't afford a mistake."

"You can't afford a mistake, but I can. I'll return the money."

"How about I send another job toward the bitch sleeping at your place right now."

"Don't you dare."

"Now you get my point. Obviously, you can't easily replace her with another. So get on and finish the job."

"I need more time."

"Your target is on the move now. The location has just been sent to you. The faster you get this done, the sooner you'll be free."

Jett mumbled some profanity and returned to the apartment. Madeline was still asleep. He grabbed his jacket and left.

***

Madeline woke on the sofa. The clock on the wall stared at her. She was unbelievably tired. She sat up and saw the food Jett had left for her on the table.

The apartment was plain and in need of decoration. Obviously a rental. Or maybe Jett just lived a simple life. He had always been like that.

Madeline shook her head, trying to clear the cloud in her mind.

He psychic ability was still not working.

She got up from the sofa and put her jacket on. She flipped her wrist unit over and saw a tiny red button she had never before thought to press.

She pressed it.

A round beam of light appeared. She was scared at first, but then she realized it was just the holocast technology—an exclusive teleport means to which she had access.

She wrote a note to Jett. "I'm going home to my children."

She stood, glanced around the apartment one more time, and stepped into the holocast.

CHAPTER 23

Ciaran slammed his foot down on the accelerator and glanced at Arik in the passenger seat. No reaction. When he had first met Arik, they'd gotten into a car chase. Arik had spent the entire time yelling at him and asking him to slow down. But now, he just stared out the window.

He figured speed was Arik's friend right now. It helped calm his emotions, although Ciaran thought Arik had handled things quite well.

They had just left the morgue. He had given Arik the news about his parents' death, not anticipating he would want to see their bodies.

But he was within his rights to ask, so he went to the police to identify his parents.

Since then, Arik had said nothing.

"Where are we, Michael?" Ciaran asked.

From the back seat, Michael said, "Very close. If we stay at this speed, we'll get to the target very soon." Michael was holding the tracking screen for the bug Ciaran had planted on the white van. The signal had been triggered right after they left the morgue.

"Great!" Ciaran said and drove even faster. "When we get there, I want you to stay in the car. Got that, Michael?"

"Sure."

They soon approached an industrial area and entered an abandoned multilevel parking garage. Ciaran drove up the ramp slowly, keeping an eye out for the white van.

On the third level, there it was, parked on the platform, out in the open. Next to the van stood the elegant woman Ciaran had met previously. She appeared to be by herself, but he couldn't be too careful.

He stopped the car at a distance. "Stay inside the car and duck down, Michael."

Michael was about to protest, but seeing the look on Ciaran's face, he decided to remain silent and slid to the floor of the car.

Arik got out of the passenger side and locked eyes with the woman. He knew she had seen his father before he was killed. He knew they'd had some kind of connection in the past. He knew only what Ciaran had told him.

But there was more.

The woman eyes glimmered with tears.

Arik had his hands shoved in his pockets as he gazed at the woman. "Ciaran said you saw my father before he was killed."

"And I saw your mother, too. I'm sorry about your parents' deaths."

"You triggered the signal. How can we help you?" Ciaran asked.

Tears started to stream down the woman's face, and she started to speak in French.

"Lady, I don't speak French," Arik said.

"She said she's sorry, and she didn't know what to do. She loves you," Ciaran said.

"Excuse me? I don't even know you!"

"I'm Bridget. I'm your mother."

"That's insane."

Bridget approached.

"No, you stay right there. Diana is my mother."

"I didn't give birth to you, but you have my son's heart. You have my blood."

"What the fuck does that even mean?"

Bridget approached again. "Please...hear me out."

"No!"

"Bridget, step back please. He said no," Ciaran said.

Bridget continued to approach. "You're the dragon," she said. "Dragon heart."

She raised her hand. Ciaran didn't see a weapon, but it seemed like a needle had been pumped out and had struck Arik's chest.

"I'm sorry, Arik," said Bridget.

Ciaran pulled out his gun but then felt a prick in his neck. He grabbed the needle and pulled it out, but not before his world started to spin. His gun fell to the ground.

Bridget pulled out a round pad. She approached Arik, who was already on the ground.

Then Ciaran heard a roaring engine. From the lower ramp, Jett flew up on his motorbike. While still airborne, he sprayed bullets from his machine gun at Bridget. He landed next to her and snatched the round metal pad she was holding.

Before Jett could drive away, a shadow darted past Ciaran.

Michael slammed a two-legged kick at Jett, sending him backward, rolling on the floor. The machine gun dropped and spun away.

Michael pounded on Jett.

Ciaran tried to stand, but his movements were slow. What Bridget had shot him with might have been just a low dose of sedative. But it was effective.

What she'd shot Arik with was something entirely different. Ciaran darted over to him, leaving Michael to fight with Jett.

Arik wasn't breathing.

"Cardiac arrest," Ciaran muttered. He punched Arik's chest. "Come on!" He did it again. No response.

He scrambled over to Bridget, who was gasping for air on the floor. He pulled a hairpin from her head and scrambled back to Arik. He jabbed the pin into his chest.

Arik gasped and seemed to resume his breathing.

Ciaran's head jerked up when he remembered that he'd left Michael fighting one of the most lethal assassins in his business. "He'll have another gun, Michael!" he warned.

Ciaran aimed his gun at Michael and Jett, but it was too late. Jett had pulled his second gun and pointed it at Michael.

"Let him go," Ciaran said.

"Put your gun down, Ciaran."

Ciaran obeyed.

Jett nodded. "I'd normally follow this up with a lethal shot to guarantee my safe getaway. But you've already hurt your wife enough. I don't want to cause any more damage by killing you."

Jett jumped on his bike and drove away.

Arik sat up groggily. He crawled toward Bridget. "What did my father do to get himself killed? What about my mother? What did she ever do to you? What about my sister? Why did you want to kill me? Tell me."

He shook Bridget, who was gasping out her last breaths.

Ciaran pulled him away from Bridget. "Give her some space. Let her talk."

Bridget reached out for Arik's hand. He withdrew. He looked as if he would strangle her if he could.

"Before your mother died, she wanted you to forgive them, whoever they are," Ciaran said.

"You're just saying that—"

"No, Madeline read your mother's last thought."

"Please!" Bridget reached her hand out again.

Arik reluctantly let her hold his hand.

"My husband was one of the founders of the Tri-Sun. He invented the Dragon. But we couldn't go...through...with the project. Because others wanted to use...the Dragon for power. They're...evil. He put the...Dragon into our son...and burned down Tri-Sun. I asked Quinn to save our son... He just told me...now...that our son didn't survive...so he put...the Dragon into ... you. It's coming, Arik... Don't let it get...get..."

Then she stared blankly into nothingness.

CHAPTER 24

Madeline strode into the familiar grand corridor leading to her chamber in Eudaiz. The light powered by Eudaizian energy shone on the polished metal pathway. It glowed a bit brighter as she walked past, and dimmed down when there was no more movement.

Screens on the wall came to life as she walked past, flashing welcome messages. She used to think the machine was humanized and friendly. But she was wrong. It was Ciaran's design, his way of saying "*You and every organic cell in your body have been scanned and verified by our system.*"

She sighed and turned toward the last door, which led to her children's chamber.

"Madeline, welcome home!"

She rolled her eyes. Behind her was Robert, their home robot, created in human shape and size. He was a learning machine, and sometime his sense of humor was too much for her to take.

"I'm in a hurry."

"I can report that you are in a negative mood. There is a trace of human sensation affecting your nervous system in a negative way. It is counterproductive—"

"I don't care, Robert."

"Affirmative. I can also report that your body mass index suggests you have lost weight and there is a trace of—"

"Robert!"

"Yes, Madeline."

"How many times have I told you I do not like being scanned?"

"Yes, but there is a trace—"

"I don't care. Keep your report to yourself. Or email it to Ciaran if that's the way your technology works." She strode ahead.

"Yes, Ciaran LeBlanc, Sciphil Three, current king of Eudaiz. You, Madeline Roux, have one remaining privilege..."

She whirled around. "What did you just say?"

"Ciaran LeBlanc, Sciphil Three—"

"I know who he is. What did you just call me?"

"Madeline Roux... Command unconfirmed. Conflicting information. I have to adjust my report."

Jake, Eudaiz head of intelligence, a very young man for such important role, rushed out. "Madeline, I'm sorry. You were too fast from the terminal. I couldn't catch you..."

She glared at him and slammed her right palm on the control panel in front of her children's chamber.

"Access denied," the computer shouted out.

"If Ciaran is determined to cut off all my access, then why let me come back here?"

"You have one remaining privilege as Sciphil One."

Robert approached, the orange light on his forehead flashing. He always flashed that signal when he was confused and about to jam up.

"Don't jam up, Robert. Ciaran isn't here to fix you. What is so confusing that you are glaring orange at me? Ciaran and I had a disagreement, and he's cutting me out of his life. That's what humans—or ex-humans—do. So stay a robot. That's the best thing for you."

Robert scurried after her with his little wheels.

"Don't follow me. You're Ciaran's robot. You're supposed to take his side."

"Bypassing programs," he said. Now he was flashing a red light.

Robert had only done this once before. He skipped over his own programs and operated on a system even Ciaran didn't have authority over. On that occasion, he saved their lives.

Madeline glanced over Robert's shoulder and saw Jake rushing after her.

She said to Robert, "I accept." He immediately turned the red light off.

"Madeline, what would you like to take for your privilege? Anything except the power towers and your children."

"I can't request access to my children?"

"I am afraid not—that's in the instructions. Your children are not only precious, they are wanted by all creatures in the multiverse. It's not safe..."

"I know...I'll take Robert." She strode away, and Robert spun his wheels hard to keep up with her pace.

"Thank you, Madeline. Thank you for trusting me."

"Your robot is showing me his middle finger, Madeline," Jake said from behind her.

"I taught him that!" she said and continued to walk out of the corridor.

A short moment later, she arrived at a temporary station. Robert was handy as he handled all computer-related matter for her. Eudaizian computer systems didn't like her commands, no matter how much Ciaran had tried to adjust them.

"So Robert, what do you have that the normal system doesn't?"

"I am tracking a movement on Earth that pertains to you and Ciaran. Based on my calculations, the movement goes against Ciaran's interest."

"What do you mean?"

"There is an eighty percent chance that he is moving toward an accumulated source of cosmic energy, and with his current resources, he will not be able to survive the encounter."

"I assumed he had contacted Jake to make arrangements. He always plans ahead. He won't move against any cosmic energy without gathering a galactic amount of ammunition in all shapes and forms available to him."

"Based on my information, Ciaran has sent only one message—the one about you coming back here and your arrangements. Then he was disconnected with his tower."

"He was disconnected, or he disconnected himself?"

"He was disconnected by his sourced tower."

Now her head started to spin.

He had been injured during the fight which resulted in her leaving him behind. He had to have had his eudqi on when he was injured, and the contact had to be close to his fatal point. So close that it disconnected him from the sourced energy.

Yet he came downstairs to play truth or dare with Jett.

Calm down, she told herself. She had a plan, and she'd stick to it.

"All right, I have some data for you to analyze, Robert."

"That's what I am here for."

"By the way, what was the trace of something you mentioned before when you scanned me against my will?"

Robert popped out a small box in his chest and pulled out a piece of paper. "I had the report printed for you. It is in plain English."

She grabbed the report. "I am not technologically incompetent."

"But you're in denial most of the time when it comes to technology. We robots are important."

"I would hit you if you were human, Robert. But if I do it now, I'll only hurt my hands. I can see you're trying to wink at me. Don't try to play cute—it's not working out well for you. Whatever you are going to score here, I'll not take you to Earth."

She glanced at the report. "You aren't serious!"

CHAPTER 25

Arete landed his shiny new vehicle in Xiilok. He didn't know what to call it exactly. It was egg-shaped and the size of a horse carriage. But it had a lot more capability than a horse-powered vehicle. Of that much he was sure. He had paid a handsome bit of multiversal currency for it.

He sighed, thinking about the amount of money he had invested in this race to power—if any of his efforts would eventuate.

The triple aperture and the uniting of the three worlds was just myth—an intriguing myth that had caught his attention. Then his innocent interest turned into an investment. He had to get some kind of return from it.

The uphill battle hadn't been easy, but it kept him amused for centuries. It was dangerous sometimes, but he was immortal. What would be the worst scenario for him? Maybe he'd get killed. That wouldn't be the end of the world, would it?

He chuckled at the prospect of being dead. He'd tried several times to die. He wasn't sure if it was even possible. He kept coming back to life. He recalled something he'd watched on a screen on Earth a while ago called *Groundhog Day*. His life was pretty much like that.

He pushed a four-foot-tall, green-skinned, minor deity with huge orange eyes forward. His rank was so minor that it might not count as a rank at all. He couldn't believe Xecheron his given him this creature to replace Asana.

He didn't know what Xecheron was thinking. He was a minor god of the underworld. Wouldn't he be able to come up with something better than this? Any creature in Xiilok could kill this little deity with a mere sneeze.

In front of the cave with the stone angel wings, Arete sighed, pointed at the dome, and said, "The man was a legend. Show some respect, okay?"

The deity looked at him blankly.

"Cat got your tongue?"

The deity shrugged and proceeded toward the door. Xecheron might be right—maybe all they needed was a token body in place. When the time came, at the right moment, after they had secured the spot at the three-world merger, they could just kill off the deity.

Inside the residence, Arete found a mess. Asana must have put up a good fight before Jael and Charmine killed him. Anyway, Arete didn't mind at all. Xecheron would kill the angel couple. That would be for the best.

He pointed at the chair. "Sit."

The deity sat.

"You will remain here until I say otherwise. In a few days, there will be some movement of the land beneath your feet. I want you to hold this talisman and follow the direction it gives you. I will give you more instructions after that."

The deity nodded. Then a dart flew through the air, stabbing into his forehead. His eyes rolled back, he fell to the ground, convulsed, died, and evaporated into the air.

Arete whirled around and copped another dart. He staggered back and saw Asana walk out from a corner—looking alive and well.

"Arete, I thought we were friends."

172

"We were never friends, Asana. You betrayed me. You gave me poison in place of the primer."

"No, I gave you the true primer made of Maikoa. That potion could kill an angel, you know. But it can't kill you because you belong to the material world."

"Liar!"

"I don't need to prove myself to you. What you have now is wolfsbane, the kind that kills creatures from the material world. You included."

"I am immortal."

"Not with wolfsbane." Asana smiled.

Arete slumped to his knees. As he bent down, he pulled a knife and threw it at Asana's forehead.

Asana's eyes crossed as he fell to the floor.

"Oleander kills Amalgam creatures. I'm sure you know that, Asana."

Dinah, Jael, and Charmine stormed out from the darkness.

Arete raised his hands, seeking peace. "I'm dying. He already poisoned me."

"Damn it, Asana, do one last good thing before you die. Give me your blood!" Dinah said. "I'll pray for your soul. My father will put in a good word with—"

"Go to hell, Dinah." Asana spat out his last words and then died.

Dinah turned to Arete, but before she could do anything, he surged up from the ground.

"Look out!" Charmine shouted and pushed Jael.

Arete threw a knife, and it grazed Charmine's shoulder. The knife dropped to the floor, and the poison on the blade sizzled.

"Maikoa," Dinah grunted and darted at Arete.

He stood up straight at this point and smiled. "I told Asana I am immortal, but he didn't believe me." He smiled and pulled the knife Asana had thrown at him out. He threw it at Dinah.

Jael leaped over and pushed Dinah out of the way. The knife hit his shoulder.

Arete threw a smoke bomb and vanished.

"Father, are you okay?" Dinah asked.

"I'm fine. It's oleander. It would kill you because you belong to the material world, Dinah, but it won't kill me."

Dinah looked at the bleeding wound on Charmine's shoulder. "Mother!"

"I'm not an angel. Maikoa can't kill me. But it would have killed Jael." Charmine looked at the knife on the ground and shuddered. "So what do we do now that the first plan is ruined, Dinah?"

"I don't know. It's not easy to get creatures from three worlds to donate blood. Amalgam is particularly difficult. Creatures here are complicated. Such a waste of time. We spent all that time convincing Asana that Arete was out to kill him, just to get his donated blood." She shook her head in despair.

"Arik is the leader of the Yellow Shield tribe. Can they donate their Amalgam blood?" Jael asked.

Dinah shook her head. "They're Xiilok citizens, but I'm not sure they are Amalgam creatures. I'm sure about Asana because he drank the water in the well and became a Xiilok creature. Damn it, I know Ciaran has contacts, but we don't have the time now. I have one batch of the primer. Can't afford trial and error."

"Are you sure the primer will work, Dinah?" Charmine asked.

"It's a theory I haven't tested. But other than that, I'm sure it will work."

"Where does she get that sarcasm from, I wonder?" Jael asked.

Charmine smiled.

Dinah grinned. "I am really just your sweet child. I've never been possessed by my evil aunt, and I've never ripped the heart of a giant hulk out to kill it. Now we need to get you both back to your world, parents."

"The transitional zone, that is," Jael said. "I know you have the bracelet, but I'm not comfortable having you to cross into the magical world."

"I'm not a crystal vase," Dinah muttered.

"You are to me, darling. Always." Charmine smiled.

CHAPTER 26

Ciaran, Arik, and Michael exited the hotel via the garage door. As they approached the car, they found Adam, the new CEO of LeBlanc Pharmaceuticals New York standing next to it. Ciaran stopped Michael and Arik.

"You tagged me?" Ciaran asked.

"No, I followed Lindsay's trail and found documentation for his care of Michael. Lindsay was very careful, I must say. But unless you're alien, any transaction on Earth has traces."

"What do you want?" Arik asked.

"I've got news. I'm afraid it's not good. The police found the bodies of a mother and daughter in the bushland. It was ruled a camping accident."

"Damn it, goddamnit!" Ciaran slammed a fist into a nearby column.

Adam continued, "It's Lindsay's wife and daughter. You don't know Lindsay well, but he has taken care of you for years, Michael."

Tears fell down Michael's face. He paced back and forth, not knowing what to do.

"Thank you. Is that all, Adam?" Ciaran asked.

"I'm here to help if there is anything you'd let me do."

"You said before that this is the LeBlancs' private matter. Why change your mind now?"

"I didn't change my mind about the LeBlancs. I just didn't have the courage to offer help before. Things happened too fast in the last few days, and I wasn't prepared."

"And you've become more prepared in the last twenty-four hours?"

"I followed the LeBlancs' business for years. You might be too young to know, Ciaran, but your father offered to provide treatments we couldn't afford that prolonged my mother's life for another eight years. The additional time we were able to spend with her was precious for my family. I am indebted to your family for that. I had always wanted to work for your family..."

"You are now."

"Yes, but I can do more. I know your family is involved with more than just the pharmaceutical business."

"Be careful what you're saying, Adam," Ciaran growled.

"I understand. I can see what happened to Lindsay and his family. I checked Michael's credit card details, I traced the car and the hotel, and I know Arik's parents' death has something to do with this. I know my way around, Ciaran. Let me help."

"I think we're going to need his help, Ciaran. You being disconnected with your network here and...up there...isn't doing us any good," Arik said.

Ciaran nodded. "All right. If you could organize this project so that it is self-contained and dismiss whatever else is relevant after you finish so that the main business doesn't have any connection with this, it would be much appreciated, Adam."

"Understood. What do you need now?"

"A private lab, a long-haul private jet, and weapons."

"I only have access to *normal* weapons right now."

"Those will do."

"Do you need people?"

"Yes, but I've already ordered them. I do need someone to take care of Michael…"

"Come on, Ciaran! How much more do I have to do to prove to you I can handle this."

"I know you're capable. But you're a minor. I can't take you with me."

"I'm eighteen!"

"He was fifteen the day before yesterday," Arik said.

"I'll stay behind. I'll do whatever you say. I know you'll leave after this. I've waited seven years to see you again, Ciaran."

"All right. You have to do what I say."

"Yes."

As they followed Adam to another car, Ciaran's wrist unit beeped.

"I thought you weren't connected to any network," Arik said.

"This is private, direct connection with Dinah's unit. It doesn't connect with any network and— What have we here?"

Michael peeked at the screen. "That's gibberish."

"No, that's Morse code," Arik said.

"It's very primitive...and Earth-based. Even if it's intercepted from, say, anywhere, the message won't be easy to decode," Ciaran said.

"And what does it say, Ciaran? Is Dinah okay?" Arik asked.

"She's taking her parents home. She thinks she's got the formula for the primer." Ciaran smiled. "Wicked."

"She can fly, too," Michael said.

"Indeed," said Arik and smiled.

Ciaran coded back the message then looked at Adam. "We'll go to the lab first if you don't mind."

A short moment later, they were in the exclusive lab of the LeBlanc New York branch. Michael glanced at the equipment and yawned.

Ciaran said, "Adam, could you get someone to give Michael some training on weapon usage and safety."

"Ciaran," said Michael, "Lindsay told me you handled your family business when you were sixteen. I can't imagine I'm doing anything near what you did. So please stop playing father. It doesn't suit you."

Ciaran glared at him.

"But I guess some training would be useful," Michael said to Adam and then scurried outside the room.

Ciaran returned to Arik. "Bridget tried to cause a cardiac arrest in you, and she had some sort of a key code in her hand. I'm guessing you have some sort of ability she wanted to terminate, and that ability is artificial."

Arik walked around the room. "Cooper said the thing that got Jenny in Xiilok is manmade. When Dinah and I were at the Red Shield camp, the majority of the soldiers were robots. Many of them were Grace lookalikes. Remember my ex? Grace?"

"Yes, she has a French accent."

"She's half French. Bridget spoke French. Is my entire life a setup of some secret mobs from Europe?"

"I have a theory, but it'll take a painful test to prove."

"How much pain?"

Ciaran looked at Arik.

"All right," said Arik. "Let's do it."

A short moment later, every vein in Arik's body was hooked to a machine.

Ciaran said, "It's going to feel like you're being electrocuted. Are you sure, Arik? This is the only way I can obtain information about the electromagnetic energy in your body and brain."

"If you say this is the only way, why waste time? If I'm a stupid robot, then let's find out."

"I don't think you're a robot. It would be a lot easier if you were. Are you sure? I might need to give you three shocks to get enough data."

"When did you turn into an old man?"

"The day I—unfortunately—got to know you." Ciaran gave Arik some water then turned toward the control panel.

"Wait. If anything happens, can you tell Dinah I love her?"

"Do it yourself, even if you have to crawl out of here."

Ciaran punched the button.

Arik grunted in pain, and his skin turned almost purple. When the pain subsided slightly, he said, "Again."

Ciaran punched the button again. Arik's eyes rolled back as his body convulsed with the shock. He said weakly, "Again."

Ciaran slammed his sweaty palm on the button.

Arik's body tensed up, and then everything stopped.

The machine pinged a happy sound as the data collection was completed.

Ciaran grabbed the machine nearby and pressed the resuscitators to Arik's chest.

Once.

"Come on, you idiot, breathe."

Twice.

Then again.

Arik's pulse picked up as Michael walked in.

"You see, this is what happen when we play truth or dare at inappropriate times. I've got data to process, and you've got a job to do."

"Yes, for sure." Michael approached enthusiastically.

"Nurse him. He'll be sick for a few hours." Ciaran left for the computer.

Michael stood next to the bed. "Sure, I can be a nurse. Whatever it takes."

Arik turned to his side and vomited all over Michael.

CHAPTER 27

Dinah and Jael flanked both sides of Charmine when they flew. They descended slowly to the soft ground in the transitional zone of the multiverse.

"Here will be good enough," Jael said.

Dinah looked at her parents. "Will I ever see you again?"

Charmine smiled. "Don't be silly. When the fight on Earth is settled, and when you are settled with your man, we will certainly come and visit you."

"If we win the fight," Dinah said and looked away because right now, she had no confidence and wasn't sure of a victory. The only and most important task Ciaran had given her was to develop was the primer. She had made no progress and had ended up having nothing for Ciaran. She shook her head.

"Where is your sarcasm? Where is your confidence? You can do this, Dinah. You know the formula of the poison. And with that, you can kill the most prominent enemy in the Cosmos."

"I have plenty of poison. I can kill with poison. But what we need now is a primer, not the poison. Whoever is jumping through the aperture will need this primer to survive. It's okay if Arete jumps. He can die and rot for all I care. But what if Arik is the one who has to jump?"

"You don't know that, Dinah."

"No, I don't know. But his brainwaves have been manipulated for a long time. Ciaran just texted me that his parents died, and it has something to do with the aperture. I guess Ciaran isn't aware of the merging worlds."

Charmine nodded. "Yes, it's easy to compound poison, but it's almost impossible to compound the primer."

"I'll see what I can do," Dinah muttered.

She embraced her parents one last time and took them toward the gateway.

"Why the hurry?" Arete spoke from behind them. He walked out with a creature that looked like a skeleton with a piece of black fabric wrapped around it.

Dinah could hear her father hiss audibly when he saw the skeleton figure.

"What do you want Xecheron?" Jael asked.

"Oh, I don't have in introduce you two? That saves time." Arete said.

"What do you want, Xecheron?" Jael repeated.

"One of your women. Your choice of which one I take and which one you keep."

Saying nothing, Jael spread his wings and charged at him. Xecheron raised his arms, spread out his three pairs of bat wings, and flew at Jael.

Then, in front of Dinah, Charmine and Arete became a whirl of black and white light, a funnel of light and wind.

Dinah had no magic, no knowledge of it at all. She wasn't sure what they were using to fight.

The wind died down quickly. Jael and Xecheron were separated, thrown apart by the opponent energy. They fell backward. While

Xecheron seemed to have no problem getting back up, Jael was suffering.

"Power from the underworld. The skeleton is a condemned minor god. Your father had no chance," Charmine said.

"If he's condemned, how can he be stronger than Father?"

Charmine said, "Xecheron killed an angel before and was condemned for it. This is the transitional zone of no authority. He can do whatever he wants here. If he kills another angel, he can't be punished for the same crime twice."

"How stupid is that rule?" Dinah exclaimed.

"Jael never agrees with me. But, angels aren't good in making policies."

Arete scurried behind Xecheron.

"Coward," Dinah muttered. As Xecheron rose from the ground, becoming bigger by the second, Dinah knew what she had to do.

She let go of her control and let the evil spirit of her aunty take over. Unlike the last time when she had no awareness of what she was doing, this time she could see herself doing it. She knew exactly what she needed to do to get reward.

She could see the world around her shudder from the evil of the spirit that possessed her. She raised her arms, pointing them at Xecheron. From

188

her mouth, a string of spells came out, spells so powerful they stopped Xecheron in his tracks.

She made a fist with one hand and then pulled it back.

Xecheron's chest exploded, and in Dinah's hands was a bleeding heart.

Dinah withdrew her hands and dropped the heart. She looked at the bleeding heart until it stopped beating.

She was in control of he emotion, her mind and her body. She was aware that had just used her evil spirit to kill evil. She had turned her weakness into a weapon.

She turned and looked at her parents to show them she was in perfect control of her mind and body. Xecheron deserved to die. She could only help.

Arete threw a smoke bomb and vanished again into thin air.

"Are you okay, Jael?" Charmine asked.

He nodded.

"He got away. Arete is the evilest character in the Cosmos. Now he got away again." Jael put his head in his hands.

"I'll kill him," Dinah said.

"How?" Jael asked.

"I need the primer."

Jael asked. "You have already had my blood. That's the blood from a magical creature. Can you make something of it? Do you really need blood from Amalgam and material world creatures?"

Dinah nodded.

Charmine pulled out a small knife she always carried.

"Don't, Charmine!" Jael said.

"What if Dinah is the only one who can deal with Arete?" Charmine asked. She turned toward Dinah and used her knife to cut her own hand. As the blood dripped, she signaled for Dinah to use her jar of potion to catch it.

"I, Charmine, from the tribe of the North Wind multiverse travelers, now announce myself as a creature from Xiilok. As a Xiilok creature, I am an Amalgam creature forever. Here is my blood, the blood of a free spirit. Take my blood and use it with good intentions."

Dinah looked at Jael and saw the devastating look on his face. But he composed himself quickly.

"Charmine can never be an angel after this. That makes my role as the angel of light meaningless." He looked up and raised his hand in oath, saying, "I shall resign from the role, return the power to the gods, and declare myself as an Amalgam. I will travel with my wife for eternity."

Jael and Charmine both turned and looked at Dinah. They smiled at her, and the trio embraced. A moment later, Jael took Charmine to the light gateway that had just opened for them.

Together, they stepped into the light, looked at Dinah one more time, and departed.

CHAPTER 28

Dalat was a beautiful highland city in the south of Vietnam. Ciaran could see why it was referred to as a French settlement city. The French architecture was prominent in almost every major construction in the city. The streets had French names, and the shops were primitive, small-scale versions of those in Paris.

They flew the jet up to the city and so had missed the major scenery. But he was sure they would have a chance to visit later when everything settled.

They stayed at an exclusive villa. Arik needed a bit more time as he had not yet regained complete consciousness regardless of how many times they had changed transport on the way up here.

As Ciaran turned around to leave the room, he stirred.

"Arik, how are you feeling?"

"Well, you're here, so I'm definitely not in heaven."

Ciaran chuckled. "I take it you're feeling well. We're in Dalat, a city in the Vietnam highlands."

"What? How long have I been out?"

"Long enough to delay everything. Do you want to sit up?"

"Sure." Arik pushed himself into a sitting position.

Ciaran returned with a needle. "This is just nutrition. You can have solid food if you feel up to it. But if you want to chuck, don't do it on me."

"Did I do that already?"

"Yes...on Michael."

"I must be his favorite person on the planet."

"That's about right. He's not liking me much now because I wouldn't let him carry weapons. Which will make it a lot easier when I leave him after this."

"Are you serious?"

"Yes. Not only is he fifteen, he's an absolutely normal human being. Look at how you and I turned out. I don't want that life for him."

Michael entered the room. "How are you feeling, man?"

"Sorry I vomited on you."

Michael sneered. "You were such a baby!"

Arik laughed. "So, after much effort, what's the conclusion about my make, Ciaran. Am I a robot?"

"No, you are not a robot. But your human body has been changed. Biologically, you are the same. But the electromagnetic energy in your body has been manipulated. That's why you're ultrasensitive to sound frequencies. And that could also explain some of the time traveling and the way your body handles light energy. In a nutshell, you could be an energy source."

"You mean like a battery?"

Ciaran chuckled. "Pretty much. Give me a few more hours. I'll have a full profile of what kind of creature you'd make."

"Well, what about a dragon!" Arik said.

Michael's eyebrow winged up. "Really?"

Ciaran shook his head. "Dragons only exist in children's fairytales. I can assure you whatever we're dealing with now isn't a fairy tale. We'll find more information when we get to Tri-Sun."

"I thought you said it burned down," Arik said.

"The headquarters burned to the ground, but we'll go to an abandoned branch. I'm sure I can make use of their database. That's the main reason we came here."

"Okay," Arik said and got off the bed.

The light in the room flickered a few times.

Ciaran grabbed Michael, pulling him inside. Near the door, a small light beam opened and flashed, and Dinah jumped out. She was a bit disoriented, and one of her wings spread out and hit the ceiling fan.

"Ouch." She withdrew the wing quickly, and it hit a gigantic decorative vase on top of the fireplace.

"Wow, nice wing." Michael caught the vase before it crashed.

"Sorry. I travel too fast." Dinah grinned.

"Dinah." Arik approached and pulled her into his arms.

She looked at his arms and saw that some of the veins were bruised a muddy gray and purple. She shrugged out of his embrace. "What's this?" she asked and then saw more on his neck.

"He was electrocuted," Michael said.

"What?"

"What matters here is that I am alive, and that I might be a dragon. Isn't that right, Ciaran?"

"You know my views about the dragon part. And I don't think that would calm the mood of your lady here. Dinah, he received three doses of electric shock so that I could test his electromagnetic energy. A woman who claimed to have something to do with his past attempted to put him into cardiac arrest and terminate him with some kind of key code. She called him *dragon* before she died. I suspected his electromagnetic energy had been manipulated."

"Do you have any results yet?"

"I need a few more hours. What's the news on your end?"

"Good news or bad news first?"

"Bad news," Arik said.

"Good news," Michael said at the same time.

"Your choice," Ciaran said.

"The bad news is that it seems that Arete has manipulated a lot in multiversal space, arranging for some kind of merger between the three worlds."

Ciaran frowned. "The material world, magical world, and Amalgam world? I read about that in Eudaiz."

"Yes, that's it. It seems Arete has tried to manipulate the creatures in different worlds to take prominent positions when the merger occurs. I think it would be in the form of the apertures. That was why he was hunting and recruiting everywhere—he was trying to find those that could survive a jump through the aperture."

"He wanted people to jump?" Michael asked.

"He isn't that kind. I think he wants to use whatever they've got to develop a mutation primer. When the merger occurs, he'll ask creatures to hold positions in different worlds, but he will take the primer and jump."

Ciaran nodded. "The jumper will have the ultimate power. "I'll bet his idiotic associates will believe him and not realize world merging is a myth."

"I don't think it's a myth, Ciaran."

"Says who?"

"My father."

"Who is an angel!" Arik said.

"This is serious business. It isn't for everyone," Dinah said. "If it was a myth, Arete wouldn't have spent centuries building it up. Hundreds of years ago, my father and several others were humans, and they jumped what they thought was the light. I think it was the aperture."

"So Jael survived. Like me," Arik said.

Dinah nodded. "Arete, Asana, Roallix, and several others jumped. That was why Arete was searching everywhere for those who jumped the aperture. I think the time of the merger is creeping close, so he panicked and pushed things ahead— and made a mistake. Still, he ran. I don't know what his next step is, but I'm sure it has to do with people here on Earth."

"I'm ready for the good news now," Arik said.

"I know the formula for the mutation primer."

"You do?" Ciaran smiled. "What do you need to make it?"

"Oleander, wolfsbane, and maikoa that grew in Xiilok. Plus blood from the creatures from the angelic, Amalgam, and material worlds. I have the first two handled. Now I need blood from a creature from the material world. The stronger the person is, the better the potion will be. That makes the perfect creature *you*, Ciaran."

Dinah pulled out a syringe from her stash of needles and gave it to Ciaran.

"How much blood do you need?"

"No, there has to be a ritual. When my parents gave me the blood, they had to recite some kind of vow or declaration of the kind of creatures they are."

"Dinah!"

"Yes, Ciaran."

Ciaran stuck the needle into his vein and drew blood. "Do I look like the kind of person who performs rituals?"

"No, but it doesn't hurt to do so."

"Well, it hurts my ego." He smiled and gave her the blood. "I'm sure my blood will be the same whether I perform a ritual or not. Trust me."

"Thanks."

Arik winked at Dinah.

"Now I need a lab."

Ciaran smiled. "I never thought of that." He pulled out a cell phone.

"That's an Earth communicator!" Dinah said. "I thought you would have connected back to Eudaiz by now to get your resources. Can you use real equipment for this?"

"This is what they call a cell phone on Earth. It's primitive, but it works. And no, I haven't yet connected to the multiversal network."

While Ciaran called his Earthly associates, Dinah asked, "You think he hasn't called Eudaiz because he had a fight with Madeline?"

Arik shook his head. "I think he's saving the best for last."

CHAPTER 28

"**A**re you sure Dinah can handle the potion herself?" Arik asked Ciaran as they stood in front of an abandoned office block outside the city.

"Since when do you doubt her capability?"

"I don't doubt it. I'm just worried."

Ciaran nodded. "I totally understand. You have a lot more to lose now that you love her."

Arik shrugged. "There's nothing you can do about Madeline? It doesn't sound like you at all."

"She walked out on me. She made her choice. What do you suggest I do?"

"Got it!" Michael grinned and pushed opened the rusty door on which he had just broken the lock.

Ciaran looked at Michael suspiciously. "I believe the LeBlancs have been giving you a generous living allowance so that you no longer have to perform the tasks you did in your previous profession."

Arik chuckled. "I didn't know your previous profession had to do with thievery."

"I didn't need to do this today. But old habits die hard, and my skills are pretty sharp." He grinned and gestured them in.

The interior of the premises was dusty. There was broken furniture everywhere.

"Someone moved out in a hurry!" Ciaran muttered.

"All right, let's go see if we can find a dragon," Arik said.

After a while, they came back to the main foyer empty-handed.

"It's just not possible. They had to leave a trace," Ciaran muttered. Michael walked around, admiring some old photos on the wall of team sports and corporate events.

"It seemed like it was a good workplace," Arik said.

Ciaran stood staring at the wall.

"Apart from thirty years' worth of dirt, what's wrong with this wall?" Arik asked.

"What does the logo look like to you?" Ciaran asked.

Arik looked at the three round circles on the wall, all intersecting one another at the center.

"Well, philosophically speaking, I think it might be the three worlds that Dinah was talking about merging. But you said that's a myth, right?"

Ciaran contemplated. "I don't believe in the three-worlds-merging theory. But each circle looks like an eclipse. An eclipse is an astronomical event, and there's nothing magical about that."

"It's a total solar eclipse," Michael said.

Both Ciaran and Arik looked at him.

"What's wrong with having an interest in astronomy?"

"Nothing. On the contrary, it's a very good interest. I like it," Ciaran said.

Michael smiled and said, "Each circle does look like a total solar eclipse. But as far as I know, this planet isn't multi-sun."

"You're saying there are multi-sun planets?" Arik asked.

"Absolutely!"

"Or the eclipses occur in multiple dimensions of time and space. And on this occasion, the dimensions line up, so we have three solar eclipses," Ciaran said.

Michael winced. "My interest in astronomy doesn't stretch that far. But it sounds like an interesting theory."

Arik nodded. "The triple eclipse theory actually ties in with the three-world-merging theory. From the multiversal perspective, creatures in the magical world might use the explanation of the worlds merging more comfortably than multidimensional triple eclipses."

"So we've been asking about the same thing, one event," Ciaran muttered. "This company Tri-Sun now makes perfect sense. Tri-Sun—or triple solar eclipses. They knew it all along. But who are they, and where on Earth can we see the triple eclipse?"

"And we still haven't found a dragon!" Arik said as he paced around the room hoping to find more clues.

"We can see the eclipse in Ha Long Bay tomorrow," Michael said.

Ciaran and Arik turned and saw Michael waving a small flyer. "I got this ad from the hotel. Best spot for an eclipse observation tour. I thought it was interesting, so I kept it."

Ciaran looked at the flyer. "It's an hour and a half flight from here. Let's go."

"I thought it'd take two hours," Michael said.

"Not on a private jet, Michael," Arik said. "We'll pick up Dinah on the way there as well?"

"Yes, Arik. We're going nowhere without Dinah."

Soon, they arrived at the lab and saw Dinah rushing out with a big grin on her face.

"I love that brilliant smile!" Ciaran said.

Dinah held up a syringe. "A success!"

"One dose?" Ciaran asked.

"Yes, Ciaran. And it should be injected just before the individual makes a jump through an aperture. This potion will aid in the transformation process and help the person survive the energy surge and arrive at the other end of the aperture as a new and powerful creature."

"Can a person survive triple apertures?" Michael asked.

"I'm not sure. I'm working on a theory that creatures can jump one aperture at a time because only one of them occurs at a time."

Ciaran shook his head. "Actually, the jumper of the triple apertures will only have to jump once, right after the three eclipses line up."

"Three eclipses? What am I missing?"

Arik smiled. "I'll explain it to you. But right now we have a flight to make."

The group boarded the airplane, and the private jet took off.

"Still not calling Eudaiz, Ciaran?" Dinah asked.

"I'll call when the time is right." Ciaran instructed the pilot to land in a nearby town. "It's better to survey the inland first. Then we can go to the water a little later. My people will organize what we need by the water."

They landed at a small airport in a rural area.

"Great location. Very peaceful. How are we going to get to the water from here?" Arik asked as he looked at endless rice paddies divided by small clay borders and bamboo fences.

Ciaran and Dinah focused on their electronic devices to navigate and plan.

"I'll arrange transport," Michael said and scurried away.

A short moment later, they heard Michael yelling, whistling, and making all sorts of strange noises to try to get the two animals in front of a cart moving.

He didn't seem to be communicating well with the animals.

"I should have paid for bigger donkeys," Michael said.

Ciaran laughed.

Arik said, "They're not donkeys, they're buffalos, Michael! They're not good transportation because I can walk faster than they can. Where did you get them?"

"The village over there." Michael pointed.

"I'll get some real transport," Arik said and went into the village.

A moment later, he was back.

Ciaran looked up from his electronic device. "What in God's name is that thing, Arik?"

"It's pretending to be a motorbike. Are you taking it or not?" Arik adjusted his long body on a small scooter which appeared to be green beneath a thick layer of clay and dirt.

In the distance, they heard the engines of monstrously big motorbikes growing closer. Ciaran grinned. "That's what I want."

He turned around and saw a group of goons riding motorbikes, zooming on and off the rice paddies, destroying the crops and headed directly toward them.

"They aren't my people!" Ciaran said.

CHAPTER 29

Jett stopped his motorbike and locked eyes with Ciaran. The group of local gangs in front of Jett stopped their motorbikes and had their hands on their pockets with guns hidden. They waited for Jett's signals.

"Wrong guys," Jett said.

"What?" a goon asked.

"I said these are not the people we're looking for. Go back into town and wait. I'll go back to the boss and get more information."

"But they've seen us!" another goon said.

Jett growled. "People have eyes. Of course they can see you. Are you going to shoot all of them? And if you lose me my job and my money, I'll put a bullet in that stupid head of yours. Now go!"

The gangsters turned around and drove away.

"Madeline is destined to have her heart broken!" Jett muttered, glancing at Ciaran once more before driving away.

A short moment later, Jett entered an abandoned warehouse, where piles of containers were stacked up to the roof of the building. There was a dark blue container with an x-mark on the door that was open.

Inside, a robotic voice said, "Verification needed."

He placed his thumb on a small panel which had just opened on the wall.

"Verified," the voice said.

The container shuddered slightly and then moved. He had been here before but could never sense the direction of the movement. It seemed to drop down a long distance, then move sideways, then ahead. He could feel the extremely fast speed when the movement was horizontal. With about fifteen minutes traveling time, he guessed the destination was a fair distance away. Each time, the paths changed. He had had a real sense of the location.

The container came up a fraction and opened to a massive polished concrete floor, buzzing with activity. People rushed around, working on machines he had never seen before. He saw endless rows of computers, strange-looking equipment, and stacks of weapons.

Is this the preparation for World War Three? He had been here before but had never seen the place operated on such a large scale, and he had certainly not seen so many weapons.

He turned into the main office. His usual contact, the man who called himself TD40, turned around and smiled at him. Now Jett noticed the movements of TD40, and they seemed a bit robotic. But he couldn't care less if TD40 was a robot or a fifty-year-old businessman as long as he got paid.

TD40 gestured toward a man standing next to him—a tall, formidable man with dark hair and striking blue eyes. There was something in his eyes that made Jett uncomfortable—the tenacity of a predator.

"This is Hoyt. He just took over the business and is your new boss," TD40 said.

Jett shrugged. "I'm a contractor. I don't care. My work's done here. As for the new part, I don't want to do it. If you pay me for the installment of the code pad I took from Bridget, I'll get out of your hair right now."

"Why hurry?" Hoyt asked.

As soon as this man opened his mouth to speak, Jett knew instantly he should leave—with or without his money.

"I have a new job for you, and it pays triple."

"No."

Hoyt smiled. "No one has refused my offer before."

"I don't think any part of my answer is confusing."

"How about immortality?"

Jett chuckled. "If I take a bullet in my head, I'll be immortal in the memory of my loved ones. Wait, I don't have any loved ones. So the answer, again, is no. Pay me, and I'll leave."

"Well, that's not up to you. I'll pay you because that's part of good business conduct. But there is no part of the business deal that says you can leave. Am I correct?"

Jett didn't know what to say, so he glanced at the exit and surveyed his escape hatch. "How long do you want me to stay?"

"Until we settle everything. We can't risk you run around revealing our location to others. But it won't be long. Just a few more hours."

Jett nodded. "I can wait. But I won't do any more work." He glanced at soldier-like people walking around a red open space. He was sure they were robots.

There wasn't a single window in this place, and he had no idea whether they were in the air, underground, or on land.

Having no option, he stood aside to observe the buzzing activities.

He noticed a symbol of three circles on the central wall. It looked interesting. He might have seen the symbol somewhere, but he couldn't quite recall.

CHAPTER 30

Arik gazed at the magnificent sight of Ha Long Bay and understood why the site had been considered a world heritage. The water was so still it mirrored the three thousand rock islands scattered around the bay. The gigantic rocks looked as if they hovered above the water. Some stood pointing straight to the sky, some looked like stone lanterns, and some just looked like dinosaur eggs.

"There is no map of this area!" Ciaran muttered, looking at his computer.

It wouldn't surprise Arik a slight bit if tourists got lost among the elusive islands.

They were on a private tour boat for several reasons. The jet boat Ciaran had arranged for made a lot of noise, and since he wasn't sure where to go just yet, he thought it best they pretended to be tourists. Ciaran wanted to survey the bay before he could plan specific action.

Michael sat at the back of the tour boat, looking as if he regretted coming.

Occasionally, a tour boat cruised past. After that, the water returned briefly to its tranquility. Astronomy enthusiasts had gathered on small cruise boats, jet skis, rowboats, waiting for the moment.

All these innocent people thought they were about to observe a total solar eclipse, not a three-dimensional multi-world war where anything could happen.

Legend suggested that the locals had used these elusive islands as hiding places during the war. The enemies couldn't find them, and sometimes, locals got lost among the islands and were never seen again.

It was impossible to imagine a battlefield of creatures from the multiverse about to assemble here, where technology clashed with magic, and humans clashed with aliens. He couldn't visualize battleships and space creatures flying around while small local fishing boats and tourist boats floated peacefully on the bay water.

"Do you know what Ha Long Bay means?" Dinah asking, looking at the translator in her wrist unit.

He turned around, looked at her beautiful face, and smiled.

"It means a place where the dragon descends," she said and smiled back at him.

"Wow, that explains all the dragon talk. But I can't see myself growing a tail or scaly skin."

Ciaran stepped out from the cabin. He hadn't talked much since the incident at the rice field.

"You could have cut his head off right in the open rice field, Ciaran. We saw what you can do on the hilltop. You chopped the hulk's head off with your mind blade," Arik said.

"He turned around to face me. I don't attack from behind."

Arik shrugged. "Whatever you say."

"It's coming," Michael said from the back, pointing at the sky. They could see the shade of the sunlight darken a bit.

"It's a cloud," Arik said.

"Dimensional shift. Be careful. Movements in the water. Michael, come to the front," Ciaran ordered.

Michael scurried to the front of the boat.

"Are you sure you don't want to connect to the Eudaiz network yet?" Dinah asked.

Ciaran nodded. "My men are here on several islands. We should be fine for now."

"I'm not supposed to see them, am I?" Michael glanced around. "Look out!" Michael shouted and pushed at Ciaran. They both fell to the floor.

A metal arrow carrying a small rectangular leather case stabbed deep into the wall outside.

Ciaran stood up from the floor. "It's a messenger. They didn't want to shoot at me, Michael."

"How can you be so sure?"

"Because this is a galactic scale war, son, and something wants to play with me. Killing too early isn't fun."

"Did you just call me son?" Michael grinned.

Ciaran waved his hand in dismissal and took the package. He pulled out a shiny electronic device.

"An iPad?" Michael gasped.

"That's an insult, Michael. Our technology isn't that primitive," Ciaran said.

"What's an iPad?" Dinah asked Arik.

"It's like a kid's toy. When you have too much money and don't know what to do with it on Earth, you can spend money on that."

The screen flashed on, displaying an image of Cooper and Jenny.

Dinah and Arik stormed over, glaring at the screen.

"Over there!" Michael pointed at a secure-looking yacht that was moving out slowly from the fog and approaching them.

On the device screen, a man in his fifties appeared. "Ciaran LeBlanc."

"Yes, who am I speaking to?"

"This is TD40, commander in charge of the Tri-Sun group. As you can see, we have a trade to do if you're interested. Two of these people for Arik."

"I need time..."

"Five seconds."

They looked up, and the yacht was already twenty feet away from them.

Ciaran looked at Arik.

Arik nodded. "Please, Ciaran. I can do this."

"Yes," Ciaran said.

There was a thunk at the side of their boat. Men on the other boat had sprayed fumes to create a thick artificial fog to cover them from prying eyes.

Dinah rushed over to Arik, and she reached up and kissed him. "I love you, Arik."

"I love you, too."

On the other yacht, two men in uniform held Cooper and Jenny. Arik stepped onto the bridge and walked over. As soon as he reached the other side, they pushed Jenny and Cooper over and withdrew the bridge.

Ciaran glanced at Michael and nodded. Michael slid onto the floor, scrambled toward the back, and shot a tracking device onto the bottom of the yacht.

Within two seconds, a man on the other boat came out and used a device to suck up their tracking bug. He put it in the bag and shot another arrow back.

Then the yacht disappeared into the fog.

Ciaran pulled the arrow out and looked at the bag. His tracking device was inside with a small note which said, "Amateur."

Jenny and Dinah rushed over to Ciaran.

"You have a plan, right, Ciaran? That was your plan?" Jenny asked.

"You set this up with Arik, right?" Dinah asked.

Ciaran didn't answer. He turned around and hurled the tracking device against the wall, shattering it into a hundred pieces.

CHAPTER 31

The sky had darkened several shades. The crowd hummed and concentrated on the coming eclipse, and were totally oblivious to the war that was coming at them.

"You're still not calling Eudaiz, Ciaran?" Dinah asked.

He shook his head, looking up to the sky. "We don't know what they have. We can't show them what have."

"But you've got nothing here. You don't know where they've taken Arik," Jenny said, tears gleaming in her eyes.

Ciaran turned and looked at Cooper. Cooper led Jenny toward the back of the boat. "The last thing he needs now is a distraction, Jenny."

"I know. I'm sorry."

He pulled her into the only arm he had left.

Dinah approached with a needle. "Just a boost," she said.

Cooper nodded. "Thanks." He looked at Dinah. "Sorry I left in Xiilok. I went back to the hillside where they got Jenny. It was blind luck. They used the machine to scrape the hillside again, like a cycle. So I jumped right in. And they dumped me in the same cell with Jenny."

"He's got what he wanted. He's an idiot," Jenny muttered.

"Indeed, he is." Dinah glared at Cooper. "I'll ask Ciaran to make you an arm. But it will come at a cost."

"Well, as long as it doesn't cost me an arm and a leg, it should be okay."

"Not funny. Are you sure it was underground where they took you?"

Cooper nodded. "They always move in confined spaces. It could have been underwater, but judging from some bumping incidents, it felt solid, like ground. Dirt and rock rather than water."

Dinah nodded and left for the front of the boat. She found Ciaran still staring at the sky, which was darkening by the minute.

They felt a current in the air. A brush of electricity on their skin. The eclipse was closer.

Ciaran turned and looked at her. His body glowed slightly.

"Your eudqi is on?"

He nodded. "The dimensions are shifting."

"Yes, I can feel it, too."

Michael approached and saw a halo of light around Ciaran.

"I can travel across multiple dimensions. This light is the energy, my protection. You don't have this protection. Therefore, under no circumstances should you travel with anyone or any creature to another dimension. You will die."

"Understood." Michael nodded.

"Can you stay on the boat and take care of Jenny and Cooper?" Ciaran asked him.

Michael nodded again.

"My prediction is that the merger will happen in another dimension. Humans here won't see the triple eclipses. They can only see one. That might mean the war won't occur here."

They felt the boat shudder. The people on the water gasped.

"You'll come back here, right?" Michael asked.

"Of course." Ciaran said, knowing Michael didn't believe him. He had made a promise to Michael seven years ago. And he didn't keep it.

Michael nodded and went to the back of the boat.

"It's time," Ciaran said.

Ciaran's men delivered an air jet ski right at the side of their boat. The air jet ski parked, hovering in the air.

"I'll open the portal now. Will you come with me?" Ciaran asked Dinah.

He opened his portal. A beam of light flashed. Dinah said nothing but followed right behind him. Ciaran jumped onto the air jet ski and dove into the dark space, dashing around unrecognizable objects and debris.

"Where are we?" Dinah asked.

"Near Alphi. This is a possible path to see the triple eclipses."

"There." Dinah pointed to a black space with three small wedges of light around it.

They heard a howl nearby.

"That's Arete," she said and pulled out her gun.

Ciaran spun the jet ski around. He blasted his first mind blade at Arete. He had done this several times before—he could kill by sending giant blades toward his opponents using his mind power. But the blades operated on his energy, and every strike taxed him. Thus, without going back to Eudaiz to recharge, he would soon be running out of energy if he weren't careful.

Arete was hit, and judging from his grunt, it was a severe blow.

It was too dark to see much.

"I can't afford to hit randomly," Ciaran said.

"I know." Dinah jumped off his jet ski and spread her wings.

"Dinah!"

She ignored him. She flew to the dim shade of the remaining light before the total eclipse. She could see that she flew above Arete, so she fired down at him. He howled in pain and then dashed into another dimension.

"I've lost him," she said and returned to the jet ski.

"You're reckless, Dinah."

"Look in the mirror before you say that. Where did he go?"

"I don't know."

"Give me the primer, Dinah," Arete said from right behind them.

Ciaran spun the jet around and saw Arete floating in the air with Michael dangling over his shoulder.

"You bastard," Ciaran growled, but he couldn't send another mind blade at Arete because he had Michael.

Dinah jumped off the jet ski again.

"Here," she said and held up the jar containing the primer. "Come here and get it. Give Michael back to Ciaran."

Arete threw Michael at the jet ski and left Ciaran to catch him. Then he came after Dinah.

Grabbing Michael's body and holding it tight, Ciaran drove back to the human dimension. He put the boy's body on the floor of the boat when Cooper and Jenny rushed over.

"I'm sorry, Ciaran. Arete appeared out of nowhere and snatched him." Cooper said.

"His human body can't handle dimensional travel without protection," Ciaran said and shook Michael's shoulders lightly. "Open your eyes for me, son. Come on."

Michael stirred, and his eyes opened. "I'm sorry…"

"You'll die if I don't turn you into something else now. I'll give you some of my energy. Do you agree to take it?"

"You came back... You kept your promise..." Michael said weakly.

"You're dying. I'm going to inject you with alien energy, but it will change you. Do you agree to take it? Hurry, Michael."

"Can I...go with you?"

"Yes. So then you agree?"

"Yes..." Michael passed out.

Ciaran signaled. Cooper scrambled to pull out Dinah's stash of medical equipment. He found a syringe and thrust it toward Ciaran.

Michael nodded.

Ciaran pulled his shirt open, revealing his eudqi point.

"No, Ciaran. You can't afford that now," Cooper said.

"Got another solution?"

"Being from Iilos isn't too bad. I have a privilege I can use."

Ciaran nodded. "Where?"

Cooper pulled his shirt open. "Vein, next to the heart but not *on* the heart please."

Ciaran concentrated and located the faint mark of the key vein. He stuck the needle in and drew out a light blue substance. He then injected the substance into Michael's jugular.

Cooper fell to the floor, and Jenny grabbed him and held him in her arms.

Ciaran stood. He asked Jenny, "Can you take care of them both?"

Jenny nodded. "But wait, can I borrow your scanner? I want to find out how Arete found us."

"Understood. Sorry I neglected this. I'll scan." Ciaran turned on the scanner of his wrist unit. It flashed a light beam that enveloped Jenny's body.

He looked at the nape of her neck. "Here's the bug."

"Take it out, please."

Ciaran cut the small bug out with his knife and gave it to Jenny. As she stomped on it with her foot, he scanned Cooper.

"He's clean," Ciaran said. "If the bug was planted by Tri-Sun, then they're working with Arete. I should go now."

Ciaran nodded a goodbye, jumped on the jet ski again, and went back for Dinah.

CHAPTER 32

Ciaran flew into the dark space of the dimension as close to Aphil as possible. He should have told Dinah the plan. He should have discussed his thoughts and the possibility of Arete's attack from Aphil.

The prospect of Dinah fighting Arete in the dark space made his organs feel as if they were burning.

There she was. He could see her tiny shadow moving in and out of a cloud. She was paying hide and seek with Arete.

Arete was now a gigantic lump because his body was attracting any material he came across. That was the result of getting too close to the aperture without having the mutation primer.

Ciaran moved closer. He shouted at Dinah, "I'm here!"

She turned around and saw him. She flapped her wings and flew over. She didn't anticipate her wing span and spread them too close to Arete. He grabbed the tip of her wing and then a bunch of feathers.

"Ouch," she yelped.

Ciaran flew over, firing at Arete with his gun in one hand and controlling the joystick of the jet ski with the other hand. Arete turned around and whacked at Ciaran's vehicle with a tail that had formed from the concrete-like material that had adhered to his body.

The jet ski tipped over, and Ciaran fell over to one side but still hung on to a bumper bar at the back. The jet ski floated aimlessly in the air.

Dinah swung over, flew underneath, grabbed Ciaran, and yanked him off the jet ski. At the same time, Arete swung his tail again, hitting the jet ski and smashing it into hundreds of pieces.

He turned and looked at Ciaran and Dinah. Dinah flapped her wings hard to keep herself and

Ciaran afloat. Arete floated toward them. She flew backward. Arete followed.

"How can he fly like that and turn into that thing ... whatever it is?" she asked.

"He tried to mutate before he jumped. Obviously, he didn't have the right primer."

Arete floated up. He looked like a rock and was the size of a small hill now.

"All right, here's what you want!" Dinah threw the jar at Arete. He caught it with his mouth.

"Let's go back," Dinah said. As they looked back up to the apertures merging, they could see the gigantic shadow of Arete flying toward the area where the apertures had merged.

"I can't imagine what he'll do when he has the power. But at least he's only one individual. Once he's gone though, he will stop the Tri-Sun to cross, because he'd want the power all to himself."

"Unfortunately, we won't have Arete to stop the Tri-Sun for us."

They heard an explosion rumble through what was left of the dark sky. Arete's gigantic form hit what sounded like a solid substance, and he exploded into thousand of pieces.

"He should have taken the mutation primer before he jumped, not the vitamin C I gave him," said Dinah.

"Vitamin C?"

"A placebo. All good experiments have a placebo, right? I didn't cheat. He asked for the primer. That's a part of the primer." Dinah grinned.

"You're right. But you should have told me."

"You're not very good at communicating when it comes to strategies, Ciaran. Are you calling Eudaiz now, because the Tri-Sun is not a one-guy operation like Arete."

"No, I'll call Eudaiz, but not now. Not yet."

"All right, let's go back for another air jet ski. You're heavier than you think, Ciaran."

She flapped her wings, and they returned to the Earth dimension, landing at the back of the tour boat.

Ciaran rushed inside the cabin and found Cooper and Michael safe and sound. He drove the boat into a large cave nearby.

"Can you stay here, please? Don't come out no matter what happens," he said to Jenny. She nodded.

Ciaran called his associates. In a few seconds, a large air jet ski was delivered to the mouth of the cave.

The water began to rumble. Several ripples ran underneath as if something was about to surface.

"So it will actually happen here. They don't care if innocent bystanders die." Ciaran called his men and ordered them to get into strategic positions. He hopped onto the air jet ski. Dinah hopped on the back without an invitation.

"Are you sure, Dinah?"

She slid her arms around his waist and held on to him. "Well, Madeline isn't here, so I'm taking this opportunity to hit on you."

Ciaran laughed. "I'd love to see Arik's face if he heard that."

"Then we'd better make sure he's alive to hear it. Now can you tell me the plan?"

"I think the dragon is some sort of machine, and it might come up from under the water. I have my men on almost all islands here. They'll shoot the dragon into particles before it jumps into any apertures."

"What about plan B? What if your first plan doesn't work?"

"That's all I have."

They heard the sound of water cresting. People in the middle of the bay screamed. In the dim light coming from some of the boats, they could see the dragon's head emerge. The top of its head was the size of a hill. When its dozens of eyes rose above the water, they glowed green, and each eye was the size of a hot air balloon.

The dragon's head tipped a large tour boat over. People started running and swimming for their lives.

The dragon roared.

"In position..." Ciaran waited a bit longer. "And fire!" he said when the dragon's head was completely above the water. A dozen air jet skis zipped over and fired machine guns at it.

The dragon kept rising above the water. The bullets didn't seem to make a scratch. The dragon roared again.

"It is indeed a machine. Ordinary bullets won't kill it," Ciaran said.

CHAPTER 33

The dragon grew taller by the second. On the water, people and boats were running for their lives. The more chaos there was, the more casualties there were. Boats were flipped over. Lights went out. The sky grew even darker.

The dragon roared.

People cried for help.

The eclipse was almost complete.

The dragon raised a limb and wiped out Ciaran's air jet ski troop.

"Fighter jets!" Ciaran said into his communicator.

They heard the roar of fighter jets coming from different directions. They flew through the air and rained down the most lethal Earthly weapons humans had available on the head of the dragon.

It roared.

Half of its head caved in, but the damaged part grew back. Its twelve green eyes now pumped whorls of fire that surrounded the fighter jets. In a short moment, not a single fighter jet was left.

"Can you drive?" Ciaran asked but didn't wait for Dinah to answer. He slid back. Dinah leaped up and over his head to land in the front seat.

"More fighter jets. Go all in," Ciaran ordered. More fighter jets flew in. They circled around the head of the dragon and fired nonstop.

The dragon was distracted by the jets.

Using all he had, Ciaran willed his mind blade and sent a gigantic spinning steel blade toward the dragon's head. The head of the dragon was cut off. It crumbled into dirt and rained down into the bay.

Ciaran leaned heavily on Dinah as his energy had drained so quickly with the blast. The dragon's head was completely gone, but the dangling jugular vessels and wires still sparked and pumped out an oily liquid into the air.

The dragon's roar still echoed.

Ciaran wiped away the blood that had trickled from his nose and concentrated. He knew there was more to come. The fighter jets kept shooting at the body, but it wouldn't collapse.

From the gaping hole that used to be the head, another lump of meat pushed up.

"You can't be serious!" Dinah exclaimed as the head of the dragon grew again.

The new head grew quickly. Ciaran straightened his posture.

"Ciaran, how much more do you have left in your tank?"

The new head growth completed itself no matter how many fighter jets shot at it.

"It learned," Ciaran muttered. "Bring in Black Bird," he said into the communicator.

They heard the roar of an engine from hell.

"We'd better move a bit further away, Dinah."

"All right," she said and swiveled the air jet ski to get as far away as possible. The fighter jets did the same.

The dragon paused for a brief second, completing its changes. But it was too late. Black Bird descended to it from the sky, and a smart bomb was dropped right at the center of its head.

The explosion was so massive it felt as if the Earth might have cracked under the impact. But only the head was blown off. The body crumbled this time and sank into the water.

It was quiet.

Ciaran and Dinah looked up.

"Is that it?" Dinah asked.

"I don't think so."

A haunting sound tore through the dark sky.

From the water, the dragon head surfaced again.

"Is this a different one?" Dinah asked.

"This is the real dragon! They used the previous one to survey us. I'm afraid Black Bird won't work on it anymore."

"What else do you have, Ciaran?"

"Nothing here." He switched on his wrist unit. "Jake, engage RTN26."

"Affirmative," the confident voice of Jake, Eudaizian head of intelligence and Ciaran's most trusted staff member, responded.

A dimensional gateway opened. Fifty holocasts beamed out fifty giant spider-shaped jet missiles—the latest development in the Eudaizian weaponry suite.

The dragon roared.

The missiles flew at the dragon.

It roared again and grew bigger. The head spliced into multiple snake-like necks and smaller dragon heads. It grew taller and taller. The heads kept splitting until it had several hundred snakeheads, confusing the missiles.

If one head was hit, a hundred more grew.

"Damn it!" Ciaran cursed.

While the missiles tried to tackle the endless number of heads, the body grew still taller, and it started to lift from the water.

"It's going to jump the triple aperture from here," Dinah said.

"It's time. Come on, Arik," Ciaran said.

"What?" Dinah exclaimed.

"Stop firing," Ciaran ordered the missiles. They stopped firing but still hovered, waiting.

The skin covering the heart area of the dragon glowed. A round circle of light came from the fraction of the solar eclipse that remained and cut into the glowing skin of the dragon. It melted and fell off.

Inside the dragon's heart was a small chamber where Arik was tied to four poles to provide the power for the dragon. When the skin over the heart was gone, he stopped the solar light he had been drawing from the eclipse.

Lifting his head up, he looked out and saw Dinah and Ciaran on the flying jet ski.

"You'll have to catch him, Dinah."

"Catch him? Why can't we get him out now?"

"Just wait for it."

Arik yanked off the wires that bound him.

"They didn't know I installed a switch for him."

"What switch?"

"Power."

"Ciaran!"

"He agreed. You got the angel wings. He wanted a switch."

Arik went to the power source where his hands had been connected. He placed his hands against the palmprint on two separate panels. The snakeheads hissed happily as they received more power.

Arik concentrated and drew more energy from the wedge of the leftover solar light. Beams of white light streaked down to Arik's back and absorbed into the blue dot on his spine.

"That part wasn't in my plan," Ciaran said.

"My father taught him that!" Dinah said.

"I think he's trying to do more than just impress the in-laws."

"Whatever you say, Ciaran."

When Arik's back was covered in a halo of light, and the thousands of snakeheads were dancing happily, Arik swapped his left and right hands to the opposite panels.

He drew once more and pumped the light energy into the opposite panels.

The thousands of snakeheads exploded at once. The dragon head stopped moving. Its skin cracked, and the dragon's head, heart, and body exploded.

Arik was flung out into the air.

Dinah flew into the air, catching Arik's falling body and letting Ciaran handle the air jet ski.

Dinah and Arik descended rapidly. Ciaran flew under them and caught them on the back of the jet ski. The three of them flew back to the tour boat.

Behind them, the giant dragon disintegrated into millions of fiery particles.

CHAPTER 34

Ciaran hovered the jet ski next to the tour boat. Dinah brought Arik over and lay him on the floor. Jenny rushed over.

"Is he okay?"

Ciaran checked Arik's pulse. "He's fine. Just needs to rest. If three electric shocks didn't kill him, this is nothing. He'll wake naturally. No drugs, Dinah."

"Yes, Ciaran."

"How are Michael and Cooper, Jenny?"

"Sleeping like babies."

"Good." Ciaran left for the air jet ski.

"Are there more dragons to kill, Ciaran?" Dinah asked.

"There are more things I need to kill, but they aren't dragons." He jumped onto his vehicle and flew off into the dark sky.

At the other corner of the bay, he saw what he had long been waiting for.

A giant round tank containing the headquarters of Tri-Sun emerged from the water.

Its round wall slid open to reveal a building which rose, then floated, then hovered in the air.

A small door slid open on a small balcony, and a human stepped out. He was at gun point. Ciaran recognized the human. It was Jett. Before the gun was fired, Jett turned around and jumped.

Ciaran flew over and grabbed him before he hit the water. He flipped Jett over the back of the air jet ski.

"Thank you," Jett said.

"Now we're even. I don't want to owe you."

Ciaran floated the air jet ski up to the top level of the building. In the glass screen of the control panel, he saw his all-time number-one enemy—the immortal Hoyt Flanagan. Standing next to him was the man who had previously identified himself as TD40. Behind them was group of technicians, handling the control panels of what look like a spaceship.

Hoyt stared at Ciaran briefly, and then he clapped.

"I have to give it to you, Ciaran. I can't seem to get ahead of you even though I have a few hundred years on you. It must just be bad luck."

"No, it isn't bad luck. I always outbrain you."

Hoyt laughed. "You're so smart that you're letting a mercenary sit behind you right now. My intelligence suggests that you share a woman."

Ciaran smiled. "This jet ski flies only under my control. I think he's smart enough to wait until we're on the ground to kill me. And we don't share a thing aside from this flying machine."

"You're at the top of my hit list, Hoyt," Jett said.

"He's mine to kill," Ciaran said.

Hoyt chuckled and clapped again. "Look at the synergy between you two! You're bonding. Do you really think you killed the dragon and we're done?"

"Pretty much!" Ciaran said.

Hoyt continued, "That idiot Arete tested the jump with his body and the stupid mutation primer. Didn't work for him, did it? The dragon was supposed to clear the way for us. But if we don't have the dragon, we can still do it ourselves using the most advanced technology you can ever imagine. *We* are the dragons."

"Good luck!" Ciaran said.

Hoyt held up the key code. "This is the dragon key." He pointed at a giant human-sized suit standing behind him. "And that is the dragon. It's all manmade. There's no need for magical power or primer of any sort."

Ciaran smiled. "That's all you've got?"

Hoyt stopped smiling. "I enjoy our differences. But unfortunately, after I get the power, you will be the first I'm going to kill. And Eudaiz will be the first universe I'll enslave."

"I'm looking forward to it in your next life. Let me introduce you to the real version of RTN26."

Ciaran dropped the air jet ski down. Behind him, a line of giant spaceships floated up. In one of the large windows, Madeline stood next to Robert and Jake.

"Long time, no see, Hoyt. And goodbye." She raised her arm up. "Fire!"

A storm of missiles came at the dragon headquarters of Tri-Sun, shattering it into several million pieces.

Ciaran swung the jet ski over to a small island and dropped Jett down.

"I saw Madeline in the spaceship!" Jett said.

"That's correct. I know where my wife is."

Ciaran turned Jett around, pulled out a knife, and cut a small needle-sized device out of his neck.

"They bugged me?"

"They didn't do it."

"Madeline? When did she do that?" Jett rubbed at his neck.

Ciaran hopped back onto his air jet ski. "Maybe you should ask her. And thank you for leading us to the Tri-Sun headquarters. We couldn't have done it without your help."

"Hey, how the hell am I getting out of here?"

"Swim." Ciaran drove the air jet ski away, heading back to the tour boat to check on his people. He wasn't surprised to not see Madeline there.

CHAPTER 35

Ciaran leaned against the side of the boat, looking out to the bay. Serenity had returned to the water. People had cleaned up the debris and had gone about their daily business.

That was how normal life was. He wasn't sure what his life was going to be like in the future. But he was sure it would never be normal again.

Michael approached and sat next to him.

"Cooper is going to take me to Iilos."

"It's a good place, and Cooper is a good man."

"But he isn't going to be in Iilos. He said you offered him a job in Eudaiz, and a new arm."

Ciaran laughed. "Indeed, I did offer him a job. But he has to decide what to do about Jenny, I'm not taking her to the multiverse. Turning you in to Iilos is hard enough."

"It can't be that hard. I can make friends anywhere I go."

"I'm sure you can."

"So what does it take to get a job in Eudaiz like Cooper and Dinah?" Michael grinned, as innocently as he could.

"Don't stretch it, Michael."

"All right. I guess I can give Iilos a go. Do they have the Xbox or other console games in Iilos?"

Ciaran shook his head. "I'm not sure."

"What are you going to do about your wife? I'd like to meet her."

Ciaran smiled, but he was unsure how to respond, so he said nothing.

"Look who's here!" Dinah was walking out to the deck with Arik. She tried to help him a bit because he was still wobbly.

"How are you feeling?" Ciaran asked.

"I've been better."

"What's your plan now? Do you still want to lead the Yellow Shield tribe?"

Arik looked at Dinah. "I'll be wherever Dinah wants to be. The Yellow Shield can replace me if Dinah wants to be in Eudaiz."

"Of course she wants to work with me and be in Eudaiz. Am I right, Dinah?"

Dinah smiled. "I'll think about it."

***

Madeline pushed her way into the corridor leading to her New York place, a tiny apartment in the middle of Manhattan—a little shoebox that her journalist earnings could afford.

She stood in front of the door, hesitant to open it. It was too quiet for her liking. So quiet she could hear herself breathing.

Just two years ago, this was her home. It was more like a shelter than a home. She hung out with Jo, her best friend, whenever she wasn't working on a case.

She had dated many men before Ciaran. She had been in relationships. But since she had been with him, Ciaran's life, his businesses, his vision, and his friends had become hers.

Now their relationship was over. She was supposed to be back to her normal life. But she didn't know what a normal life was anymore.

Jett might be right.

What did she want?

She pushed the door open and saw Ciaran in the living room. The apartment was too small to contain the king's aura emanating from him.

The king of Eudaiz was standing in her apartment.

"Did I forget something in Eudaiz?"

Ciaran shoved his hands in his pockets. "Your children."

"You've got custody. Isn't that what you said?"

She saw the pain in his eyes, and it slashed at her heart. But there were things they had done that couldn't be undone. He had to live with it. And so did she.

"I'm ready to build a new life here, Ciaran. A normal life like any other human. I've completed my duty with Eudaiz. What else do you want me to do?"

He nodded. "I understand your decision. I just want to know if you need anything...from me."

She smiled. "What I need, you cannot give. So why ask?"

"I can't let you take the children for reasons far more important than our disagreement. Why can't you understand that?"

"Oh I do, and that's why I didn't fight your decision. I've resigned from the council and thus have no protection from Eudaiz. Our children are not humans. They are wanted by all creatures in the cosmos, and I can't protect them."

He approached her. "Why don't you give us a second chance?"

"Us?"

"All right. It was my fault. Why don't you give *me* a second chance?"

"It wasn't your fault. I walked out on you."

"Still, I ask you for a second chance."

"Ciaran, you don't mean what you just said. Ciaran LeBlanc never needs a second chance. You don't need me. Now if you'll excuse me, I'm tired and would like to rest."

He nodded and headed toward the door.

Madeline said, "At the shootout when Arik's father died, when you said that Jett had something to hide and you needed me to play along. What exactly did you expect me to do?"

He turned, squared his shoulders, and looked her straight in the eye.

"You did what was expected as the First Councillor of Eudaiz."

"But as a husband, what did you expect me to do?"

"None of what you did."

"How is that fair, Ciaran? How many women have died for you? Juliette. Sizx. Those are only two I know of. If I worried about other women, I would spend my entire life worrying."

"You don't have to worry, because those women were the past. When I'm with you, I devote everything to you and to our family. And I ask the same from you. What you have for Jett is in the *now*. And it is not acceptable."

"Ciaran, are you jealous?"

"I am a man and your husband. I'm entitled to jealousy."

"But you said my disconnection from Eudaiz contacts and all my privileges was part of the plot."

"Yes, it was."

She approached him and looked at him in the eye. "What about the divorce?"

He was smart. He would know the answer that would give him a second chance with her. He was king of Eudaiz. She was his First Councillor. They both had responsibility for the greater good, and everything was justifiable.

He looked straight back at her. "I won't lie to you, Madeline. The divorce was real."

She could see the pain in his eyes, and it pained her just as much.

He continued, "I love you too much to share you with anyone. If I have you, I want all of you, or I want nothing. If, because of that, I don't have a second chance with you, I will have to live with it. But I won't lie to you, and I won't use Eudaiz as an excuse." He kissed her lightly on the cheek and turned to leave.

"Ciaran!"

"Yes."

"Will you marry me?"

"I beg your pardon?"

"We're divorced. So let's do it all over again. Will you marry me?"

His eyes twinkled with the little spark in his eyes that happened whenever she intrigued him. She had missed that look.

He stepped back inside the apartment, tilted her chin up, and looked into her eyes. "Yes, I will," he said. "Do you have the ring?"

She pulled out the ring she wore on her necklace.

He wiped away a tear that had rolled down her face and kissed the dimple on her left cheek.

He backed her against the wall and started kissing her.

"I have one condition," Madeline said.

"All right. What is it?"

"A holiday in Ha Long Bay. All five of us."

"Five of us?"

She rubbed her tummy and grinned. "According to our very helpful robot, I'm pregnant. And he gave me the time of conception, too. Remember the New York bagels?"

He gingerly put his hand on her tummy. "So it's a normal baby. I mean, a human child. No, I mean...I love Caedmon and Lyla the way they are. But this...this ...human..."

She touched his face. "Ciaran, it's fine. I know what you mean, and I'm happy, too. Can I name our girl?"

"A girl?"

She rolled her eyes. "Yes, Robert gave me that information, too, using his wicked newly developed algorithm."

"I didn't install that program for him. He developed a baby gender algorithm himself?"

"Well, you said he's a learning machine. He's spent too much time with your little brother. And for your information, Robert asked for a reward for helping me out with the technology."

"What does he want now?"

"Apparently, he wants a smart phone to add to his collection of Earth antiques."

"Then he shall have one. And yes, you can name

our girl."

"How about Freyja?"

"What does that mean?"

"Goddess of love, sex, beauty, war, and death."

Ciaran chuckled. "Is there anything she isn't the god of?"

She wanted to answer his question, but he had stopped her words with a kiss.

No matter of how long they had been together or what they had gone through, when Ciaran kissed her, it was always like the first time.

THE END

Turn to the next page to read a short story about how Ciaran and Michael met

THE STOLEN

SHORT STORY

A SHORT STORY ABOUT CIARAN AND MICHAEL

BY D.N. LEO

Narrative Land Publishing
Narrativeland.com

The muffled scream of a child cut through the darkness.

His silhouette shook as he tried to wriggle free of the hands wrapped around his neck belonging to a large man looming over him.

One twist of the hands and the fragile bone of the child's neck would be savaged.

In a second, everything would end for the boy.

Flash.

His fury had wings. It moved as fast as light and it killed without mercy, without discrimination.

All he had to do was free it.

Today was the day he was born thirty years ago. Tonight was the night he had to kill a man to save a child.

All he had to do was to free it; his Daimon.

His father was philosophical about the Daimon. It was a spirit that was supposed to keep one righteous. But his was violent. There was nothing philosophical about violence, righteous or not.

A kill was a kill.

It was beyond reason. At least that was his father's ideology.

His father was no longer with him. Even if his father looked down from Heaven, if there was such a place, and didn't approve of his action; there was nothing his father could do about it. More importantly, he was not to live for anyone's approval. He was his own self and he was the most independent child his father had ever trained.

Independence was the first lesson his father gave him. Since he was two, his father had home-schooled and trained him to make the most of his potential. At five, his physics and his intellect excelled. And at the same time, his father discovered that his talent came with a package: violence.

The talent and the violence made the whole of him. Together, they formed his Daimon.

To his father's expectations, he had learned to utilize his intellect and had suppressed his fury. But he had never promised not to try his fury, to see what it offered. His father had said, too many times, that he was a normal human being. Well, if he was to believe that, he could just be a normal child for once; naughty and curious.

He tested his talent. And he saw what his fury did.

When he sent out a flash of his fury, he chopped

down ten old trees to the root in one swift hit. The trees Father had been talking about calling in bulldozers to clear the path to the hill, but never found time to do so.

The morning his father told him that a weird storm during the night had conveniently cleared the little bush in their backyard, he'd said nothing. *What could a four year old child do with such 'catastrophe'?*

He never let his fury out since then. For the most part, when he feared it was getting out of control, he took it out physically on inanimate objects. His furniture hated him.

He got better over the years and had learned how to control, mostly. One thing had become clear, his fury was not psychological nor was it philosophical; it was primal. It was a beast and it lived in his blood.

He inched closer into the tunnel, and the silhouettes had become more prominent, printing against the background of a fast-moving train. The noise of the train covered the scream of the child. But his mind heard the desperate scream. One second and it would be all over. He could send out his fury right now and save the child.

But, his fury would decapitate the man in front of the child.

Which was worse, dead or witness a decapitation and have blood and gore rain on him? He couldn't speak for the child.

He took over his father's corporate world when he was a teenager; and he was a predator in the business. His intellect was his lethal weapon; and he had not run into any opponents he couldn't defeat. At the same time, although he hadn't spent a day on the street struggling to make a living, nothing about human behavior surprised him. That was his basic training.

Artificial intelligence, computer science, biology, psychology, chemistry, astrology and the like. They were his toys when he was a kid.

His father swore to him that he was normal!

But now, in front of him was an extraordinary situation of two ordinary human beings. Beneath the obvious size differences of the people in conflict, the silhouettes gave him no additional information. Who was in danger here? The child? The man? Or himself? What if this was a trap to lure him into the tunnel and expose himself?

He thought he found his soul mate. She

understood him and his Daimon. She understood him and his ambition to change life and the landscape of science. She understood his pain. She thrived to make him happy and it had cost her precious life. She died making him a present for this thirtieth birthday.

Today.

Before he ran himself to the ground with guilt, he found evidence for all the objections to their marriage. He wouldn't label it the way people did, betrayal. It couldn't be a betrayal if she didn't promise him her loyalty first. They loved each other, of that, he was sure. He was even surer that he loved her.

He had run on empty for a few weeks as the world blurred by. He had a responsibility. He had people who depended on him. He had to keep going.

Today, the meeting in freezing winter in New York was a good break from his London office – a place full of painful memories. But as soon as the meeting finished, he circled back to his empty self. He didn't know where his Daimon was, but he was sure a large part of his soul was missing.

His assistant all but begged him not to go for a walk in the snow.

And here he was, standing in front of a tunnel. At the other end were the silhouettes of two people, one of whom he should kill to save the other.

All he had to do was to let his Daimon free.

One second. That was enough time to send out his fury and kill the man. It wasn't the killing decision he was hesitant about; it was who actually needed his help. He stepped further into the tunnel and yelled, "Stop!"

It wasn't the authority or the meaning of the word that stopped the man. It was the intention behind it. The intention to follow suit if the command was not obeyed. The intention to cause harm if necessary.

The man dropped the kid down to his feet.

He had walked halfway through the dark tunnel. Dim light flickered from the other end. He recalled the horror in his assistant's eyes when he said he wanted to go for a walk by himself at this hour in an unsavory part of New York.

"Who the fuck do you think you are?" The man grunted out the words.

He was only a few feet away. It wasn't the man he wanted to see, he needed to see the child. He needed to look into the child's eyes and be certain he had made the right decision.

"This ain't your fucking business. Hear me?"

He kept walking toward the child and the man. The child let out a little moan as the man lifted him up a few inches from the ground, still holding the collar of his shirt. The moan earned the child a slap in the head.

"Stop! Don't make me hurt you," he warned.

He was close enough and he could see the child's eyes now; frightened.

The man kept hitting the boy. "He's mine. I can do whatever I want to him."

There was no need to send his fury out now. He was close enough to break the man's neck with his hands.

"Let the kid go," he said.

"You're a fucking idiot. He had to earn his keep. I can't feed him forever." The man grabbed the kid and dragged him away.

"Leave the kid," he said.

The man stopped, turned around, dropped the child, mumbled some profanity and charged at him. In the dim light, he saw the reflection of a knife. He sidestepped the approach. In one swift move, the man landed on his back, still gripping the knife. The man jumped up to his feet and lunged at him again.

The man didn't give him a choice.

Years of combat training weren't wasted on him. He actually liked it for the most part. The power of body and mind control and what the human body could achieve with the appropriate manipulation of movement always fascinated him. He blocked the second attack, and before the man could thrust the knife at him for the third time, the man's knife had pierced his own throat.

Blood spurted, splattered on him and the child. The man slumped to the ground.

Dead.

He turned and looked at the child. The big brown eyes filled with tears, his small shoulders shook with fear as he stared down at the body of the man on the ground. But he didn't run.

"What's your name?"

The child blinked. "Little Mike."

"That's not your real name."

"Michael Fraser."

He smiled. "That's a lot better. Who's this man, Michael?"

"My stepfather." Michael frowned and played with the hem of his jumper.

"Why did he try to hurt you?"

"He didn't try. He just hurt me." Michael was still examining the hem of his jumper.

He lifted Michael's chin up and looked into his eyes. "Where are your parents?"

"I've never met my father. Mom died last year."

"How old are you?"

"Eight. I don't go to school, if that's your next question." Michael stared straight up at him and didn't go back to the hem of his jumper.

"Do you understand what I just did to your stepfather and why?"

Michael nodded. "He hurt me. You told him to stop but he didn't. He tried to do you with the knife, but he copped that knife in the end. He deserves it."

A cold breeze blasted his face. It wasn't the chill of New York's winter, but the tenacious tone and meaning of what Michael had said that stunned him.

He looked at Michael. "Nobody deserves to die, and no one has the right to murder."

"If you didn't kill him, he'd have killed you. Then he'd have killed me. Who would say he doesn't have the right to murder if we had both died?"

"Michael, I killed him in self-defense. That's a totally different matter. But I provoked him first. I did that because I know I can protect myself. What did you do to provoke him, knowing you can't protect yourself?"

"I told him I'd kill him sooner or later."

When he saw the grimace filling Michael's face, a chill crept into his blood. He mentally took a step back from the child. "How did you plan to do that?"

"I ain't have no planning. That was before. But I know now. If I have to kill someone, it will be in self-defense."

He crouched so his eyes were level with Michael's. "Self-defense is not a trick to get away with murder. I don't want to be the one to put that idea into your head. Perhaps, you're too young to understand, but I need to ..."

"I'm not too young. I'm eight years old. I know the most important thing a man gotta do, is to keep his promises. I keep my promises. If he didn't know how to keep his promises, he didn't deserve to live," Michael raised his voice and pointed at the dead man's body.

"Yes, Michael. Keeping promises is very important. But it's not how you judge whether a person deserves to live. In fact, you don't have the right to judge whether anyone deserves to live or die."

"So who will have a say for Nick? He got killed and he has no say. It's unfair. Nick just wanted to protect me. Just like what you did. You can defend yourself, but Nick can't. Nick wanted him to get his hands off of me and ... he killed Nick for that ...he promised my mom he'd care for us... he never did... all he did was hurt me ..." Michael's lips trembled, his shoulders shook with the chill and the emotions, tears filled his eyes but he refused to let them fall.

"Who's Nick?"

"My friend. My only friend. Nick's the one who made the money, keep the food coming in. But he's still not happy. He wanted more!" Michael pointed at his stepfather.

He could feel his blood boiling. "He killed a kid for not making him enough money?"

Tears started falling down Michael's face. "He shouldn't have bitten him ... I can take a few slaps and punches. I can take it, I told Nick that, but he wouldn't listen. He kept biting and barking until he turned around and broke his neck ..."

"Barking? Is Nick a dog?"

Michael hitched up, almost choking with his tears. "... Yes... his mom died, so my mom brought him home when I was little. He grew up fast and when I didn't have enough warm clothes last winter, he lied on top of me like a blanket."

He reached out a hand to wipe the tears on Michael's face, but the child backed up.

"He made Nick do all the tricks on the road to distract people so I can pick pockets ... days after days, nights after nights ... we were freezing, no food, no warm clothes, but we brought home the money. I promised Nick when we save enough money, I'll run and I'll take him with me. But we don't have enough yet…"

Michael shivered. His jumper was obviously not enough to keep the chill off him. He reached out to Michael, but the child once more backed out. Tears still streamed down Michael's face regardless how many times he wiped.

"We tried. But it's winter. People won't get out that much. We couldn't get much money. He cut off our food and hit me. That was when Nick got angry. I told him not to… I can take it … but he kept biting until … until he grabbed his neck and twisted it broken. … Nick can't defend himself … he provoked that man to get himself killed …" Michael gasped for air.

"He had no right to hit you. For that he would go to jail. But you can't say you'd kill him because of what he did to Nick. I understand you're upset and Nick is your friend …"

"Is this because Nick is a dog?"

He simply didn't know how to respond without digging deeper into the wound.

"I promised Nick I'm going to get him out of here. I couldn't keep my promise. Without Nick, I can't pick any pockets. Then he beat me more… and more … just now … I told him I'm going to kill him. He got angry. He's going to do what he did to Nick. He's going to break my neck tonight. But I'm ready for it... I want to see my mom ..."

Michael swayed, on the verge of passing out. He pulled at the kid and wrapped his arms around him. "When was the last time you ate something?"

"Can't remember ..."

He took off his thick coat and wrapped it around Michael. The coat was too big for the boy to walk in so he carried him in his arms. Michael's head lulled against the crook of his neck and stayed there for a short moment.

He walked along the tunnel to the main road. When he nearly got to the road, Michael stirred and straightened his head. "Where are we going?"

"Hospital. I need to put some food into you, but we have blood all over us. If we go to a food stall, they'll call the cops. So, the hospital seems to be appropriate. I want the doctor to check you out, too."

"No, go to the cops. The police station is just around the corner. We have a dead body in the tunnel and he ain't a dog."

"I can take care of that after I take you to the hospital. I'll call for a car now."

"You mean a cab?"

"No, my company car," he responded, and then remembered he had left his cell phone in the boardroom after the meeting. He must have caused his assistant a panic attack by now. "Damn it!" he cursed.

Michael laughed out loud.

"What's funny?"

"You talk pretty, so I didn't think you'd swear."

"What do you mean?"

"Your words are pretty. I like them. Mom has pretty words, too. She'd been to school for many, many years. She said she wanted me to go to school, too. She never got around to do it. We moved around a lot. Then she ran into him..."

"Did he get violent with your mother?"

Michael said nothing and leaned into the crook of his neck again. "Okay. I won't ask. Now, I don't have my phone with me, so I have to walk to the main road to hail a taxi ..."

"Police station, just around the corner," Michael mumbled.

He kept walking.

"Cabs won't go this way. You can only get them at the rank."

"Would you mind telling me where the rank is? Or I'll go to the main road and ask someone."

"They have food at the police station."

He kept walking.

"You're shaking," Michael said.

"Yes, I'm cold because you're wearing my coat."

"Okay, you'll find cabs on the left, turn there and cross that little street."

He followed Michael's instructions and ended up at the police station. He pushed the door in. A blast of warm air inside greeted them with the bonus of a dozen pairs of eyes staring at the blood on their clothes.

"Put me down, I look like a scarecrow," Michael said. He put Michael down on the floor and the coat pooled on the floor. Michael took the coat off and gave it back to him.

Seeing the blood, the officer at the front counter gave them immediate attention and got them into an interviewing room, separate from the main foyer.

"Officer, we have an incident to report, but the kid hasn't eaten for days. Could you get him something?"

One officer went for the food and another remained in the interviewing room. The first officer soon returned with a sandwich and a bottle of water.

Before he could say anything, and before the officer took a seat with his notepad, Michael said, "I found him like that in the tunnel. Dead. Blood everywhere. He said he'd get some dinner, but I waited for a long time. So I went out and looked for him. I found him in the tunnel." Then Michael pointed at him, "Then Mr. Pretty Talk found me and took me here. I was scared shitless." Michael bit into the sandwich.

He arched an eyebrow and opened his mouth to say something, but Michael cut in again. "I can sort things out with the officer here. So, you can go now."

"I beg your pardon?" he said.

"The kid said he's fine and you can go. I know the guy Michael's talking about. He's a regular here," the officer said.

"Who's the regular? Michael or his stepfather?"

"Both. His stepfather, if he deserves the title, is the worst kind of junkie. Someone is going to do him in one day. Let's hope today is the day." The officer shook his head and made notes on his writing pad.

"But I found them, shouldn't I give a statement?"

"Ciaran LeBlanc, is it? Sorry if I didn't say your name right." Michael put Ciaran's wallet on the table. "Old habits die hard."

Ciaran smiled. "Now that's pretty talk."

"Mom taught me," Michael grinned. "Didn't mean to pick your wallet. I just wanted to know your name."

"You could have asked me."

Michael took another bite of the sandwich and spoke with a mouth full, "Man, if ya told me, I wouldn't get the spelling right."

"It's shouldn't be a problem if you go to school."

Michael arched an eyebrow. "School doesn't feed me."

"You're saying if you didn't have to worry about food, you would go to school?"

Michael contemplated, but said nothing in response.

"Can you promise me if you don't have to worry about food, you will go to school? I know you're a man of his word."

Michael kept chowing down on the sandwich and shook his head. "I can do this myself. Don't need ya no more." Michael gave Ciaran a dismissive shrug.

Ciaran nodded. "All right then."

He stood up and signaled the officer to take him out. When Ciaran was at the door of the interviewing room, Michael said, "I want more."

Ciaran turned around and arched an eyebrow. "And what else would you like?"

The officer chuckled.

"I go to school, I'll need pocket money. I need to buy clothes, books and all sort of ..."

"All right, you will have an allowance. What else?"

Michael stood up and approached Ciaran. "I will give you your money back and I want it on paper. I want a man to write it down on paper."

Ciaran frowned. "You want me to give you an allowance and have my lawyer put it in writing?"

The officer's jaw dropped and he glared at Michael.

"No. I want your lawyer to write down that I owe you the money and I will pay you back when I grow up. I want to have that paper."

Ciaran nodded. "I'll send my lawyer tomorrow to draw up the paperwork." He glanced at the door of the police station and saw his company car had arrived. Ciaran nodded toward the officer at the counter, thanking him for making the arrangement. Then he turned back to Michael. "I have to go now."

Michael nodded.

"If you want to keep in touch, all you have to do is to ask me. You don't have to hang onto a piece of paper."

"Are you going home now?"

Ciaran nodded. "Yes. I am flying to London tonight."

"When will you be back here?"

"I am not sure. I'll have to check my schedule."

Michael smiled. "See! I need that paper."

Ciaran laughed. "You're a very smart boy. You'll do well at school. Learn everything you can, make a lot of money and pay me back your loan."

"I promise." Michael said solemnly, his eyes gleamed with tears. Ciaran opened his arms. Michael dove in and hugged him.

Ciaran left for the car. Before Ciaran got in, he heard Michael call out. He turned and saw Michael standing at the door of the police station with his palm open, revealing a pocket watch. Michael approached. Ciaran crouched to avoid having his six foot three height towering over Michael.

"I'm sorry. I just wanted a souvenir. Couldn't take this one. It's your father's watch." He gave it back to Ciaran.

Ciaran took the watch, rubbing his thumb on the engraved text, "The love of my life - Conan LeBlanc." He smiled. "I actually stole this from my father."

Michael eyes widened. "You steal?"

Ciaran nodded and winked at Michael.

"Did your father find out?"

Ciaran shook his head.

"You're so cool!"

Ciaran laughed.

"Will you visit me when you come back to New

York?"

"Of course, I promise. You can keep this watch if you like, as proof I will be coming back for it."

Michael shook his head. "I have your word and the paper. That's enough. You need that watch more than me."

"What do you mean?"

"In the tunnel, when I said I was ready for him to break my neck, I meant it. Nick was the only thing I had left from my mom and he took Nick from me. When you walked into the tunnel, I saw the light. Mom always said the light would come for me one day, and everything would get better. You brought me the light. I haven't said thank you for that."

"You're welcome." Ciaran smiled and slid the watch back into his pocket.

"Don't let anyone take the watch from you."

"I won't, I promise. Now get back inside, you're shivering."

Michael rushed in and hugged Ciaran tightly.

"One more thing." Michael grinned.

"What?"

"Merry Christmas!"

Ciaran had just now realized that Christmas was coming in a few days. It had never meant anything to him, until now. He looked at Michael and said the words he had never said in his life, "Merry Christmas to you, too."

Michael smiled again, then, turned on his heel, and scurried inside the building.

Ciaran stepped into the world of his familiars; inside his long black limousine. As the car left the police station behind, Ciaran saw Michael peeking from inside the door of the police station. He rubbed his thumb on the pocket watch his mother had given his father.

If he hadn't stolen the pocket watch off his father, he wouldn't have any personal item from him. The business empire and legacy his father left behind wasn't for him, but for the family. Everything his father had done was to make him a better man and to make the most out of his potential.

But he occasionally wanted to be just a kid.

Thirty years ago, he was born on this day. He thought his childhood was stolen. He thought he was lost. Today, he saved the life of a child and, at the same time, had saved a part of his soul.

In return, the child had given him the meaning of Christmas.

For all of that, he was grateful.

RANDOM PSYCHIC

A SHADE OF MIND
BOOK ONE

SAMPLE CHAPTERS

OUTLANDERS OF THE MULTIVERSE
COLLECTION

BY D.N. LEO

Narrative Land Publishing
Narrativeland.com

Random Psychic

Synopsis

Technologically incompetent Madeline has to use her random psychic ability to track down a secret identity of an avatar from the most advanced game technology on Earth, or her best friend will be killed. During the process, she falls for Ciaran, a man who possesses more dangerous secrets than the kidnapping ordeal she has already tangled herself in.

This is the first instalment in an urban fantasy thriller series, filled with paranormal romance and science fiction twists and turns!

Hate leaves ugly scars, love leaves beautiful ones.
Mignon McLaughlin, The Second Neurotic's Notebook,
1966

CHAPTER 0

She stared at the last three seconds of her life.

A red double-decker full of passengers was racing straight at her, and she couldn't do anything but stare at it.

Like the traffic and everything else surrounding it, the bus seemed to move in slow motion, but Madeline was more than certain that it was zooming in full speed in reality.

The bus was going to crush her the same way the kidnap and ransom ordeal had cut short Jo's life.

Jo was like her sister. They had grown up together, but they might not grow old together.

Madeline kept staring at the bus. It was real. It was enormous. And her psychic ability didn't seem to help at all—if she did have such ability.

Five seconds ago, Madeline had seen it—the haunting blue dot hovering in the air, giving her guidance. She couldn't believe her eyes. She was a psychic after all. The blue dot glared at her and blinked. *That's unusual*, she had thought. It had been three days that she'd stalked this place, and now her psychic ability had finally decided to kick in. *About damn time!*

She could save Jo now, and her life would be back to the way it was. Not that her life had been spectacular, but it was much better than her current situation.

The second blue dot appeared, blinking at her. She gazed at the dots, and then they were no longer blinking. They weren't blue, either, but a bright yellow.

And they came with sound.

Honking.

Shouting.

She blinked. They weren't her psychic blue dots but the headlights of a double-decker racing at her in full speed.

She glanced around. In a blur of motion, she realized she had just stepped out in front of ongoing traffic in the middle of a busy road in the center of London.

She now stood in her reality and froze.

CHAPTER 1

Someone grabbed Madeline's arm and pulled her back onto the sidewalk. The double-decker zoomed past, and the other cars kept moving. If it had been New York, she would have stirred up a hideous bout of road rage. Madeline was still dazed. She turned around and looked at the man who had just saved her life.

"Are you okay?"

"Thank you," she automatically said and immediately realized that those words she kept in her vocabulary inventory didn't exactly answer the man's question.

Then Madeline shook her head. *Focus. Stay strong. You're Jo's only hope,* she scolded herself. She turned toward the man, who was still looking at her with concern.

"I'm fine. Thank you. I'm sorry. The jetlag is killing me. And apparently, I was looking the wrong way." She gestured toward the traffic and smiled. "Madeline. I'm from New York." She reached her hand out for a handshake.

"Peter. I'm from . . . here . . . apparently." He fumbled with his briefcase, swapping it to his left hand so that he could respond to Madeline's greeting.

Madeline pointed at the building across the road. "I'm looking for LeBlanc Pharmaceuticals. But I think I've got the wrong address. That building looks more like military barracks than business headquarters."

Peter arched an eyebrow, looking Madeline up and down.

"I'm a journalist. I'm writing a business column about one of their new products. Is there a problem?" Madeline asked.

"Oh, no. No problem at all. Nobody has any problem with the LeBlancs."

Madeline smiled and waited for the next part of Peter's speech, but it never came. Instead, he shrugged. "Well, to be honest, even the locals know almost nothing about them. I'm sorry I can't help you. But I can certainly show you around if it does any good. And the I around the corner is one of London's hot spots. I'm sure it will help cure your jet lag."

Madeline smiled but cursed on the inside. Peter was a decent-looking man. She hadn't been in a serious relationship for a while—not that no one was interested in her, but her situation was too complicated to let anyone into her life. Still, it was nice to be hit on occasionally.

She was tall, slim, and attractive enough, but Madeline didn't consider herself pretty. She had a slightly long, oval face, big brown eyes, a generous mouth with full lips, and a dimple on her left cheek. A sea of brunette curls wrapped around her shoulders.

A hot cup of coffee was tempting, but now was not a good time. "I'm sorry. I've got to get this done, or my boss will be very unhappy. Thanks for the offer, Peter. Maybe next time." Madeline waved her gloveless hand goodbye and scurried away, shivering in the winter chill.

She glanced at the reflection on the shop window and saw that the smile on Peter's face had been replaced by a strange look.

She wouldn't be mistaken. She had seen that look several times. It was the look of a predator who had just lost his prey.

Instead of going straight home, she turned to the opposite direction and headed toward a crowed shopping center.

CHAPTER 2

Hours later, throwing her light backpack over her shoulders, Madeline headed toward a small apartment on a back street in Knightsbridge. Rows of terrace houses that curved along a tree-lined street looked invitingly at her. The black gothic-styled light poles and street fences accentuated the beautiful blend of modern and classic London.

She normally adored and admired the architecture. But right now, Madeline was cursing the amount of money she had to pay to stay in Knightsbridge on such short notice.

There—she saw those blue dots again.

It had been a secret she'd only told Jo, and Jo called it her psychic ability. After the incident in the bush that both Madeline and Jo didn't want to remember, Madeline had appeared to be able to see people's *minds*—or at least she thought that's what it was.

Sometimes it came from those she had been in contact with. That was how Jo speculated she was able to track down a missing person. Sometimes it randomly came from a stranger when they directed their thoughts at her. Other times, she had absolutely no explanation of where the dots came from. She wasn't a mind reader—she didn't know what the thoughts were about. She just saw them as the blue dots.

Ironically, her randomly found ability only worked when she didn't need it, like when it had led her in front of a fast approaching bus.

The dots hovered in front of her and then moved toward the alley leading to Hyde Park. After the near-fatal encounter with the bus, Madeline didn't think it was wise to follow the psychic specks anymore. She ignored them and headed home.

❉ ❉ ❉

Her cell phone buzzed as soon as she entered her apartment. She picked up the phone and kicked the door closed.

"Madeline," she answered while searching for the light switch on the wall.

At the other end of the line, a male voice croaked, "I miss you. It's been a few days. What have you got for me?"

"Zen, I almost got hit by a bus trying to get to the door of LeBlanc Pharmaceuticals. Their premises are guarded like a military barracks. Seriously, I'd have a better chance of running through the gates of Buckingham Palace to the Queen's private chamber than breaking into the front yard of that building."

"That's why I sent you there, honey. We can't compete with the LeBlancs using weapons, money, or manpower. Your little gift is just what we need."

Madeline finally found the light switch. She flicked it on and strode toward the fireplace. Her teeth were never going to stop chattering if she didn't get a fire going.

"I don't have any gift, Zen. You know I can barely operate a computer let alone hunt down a computer geek and ask him questions about an avatar."

"I saw the games you played with Jo, Madeline. Don't bluff with me."

Madeline closed her eyes. *Damn.* Jo made her play guessing games just to prove that Madeline's psychic ability was real. Jo believed in it more than she did. Since Jo was doing research on a new simulation game, Madeline thought it would be fun to help out. Now those games were biting her in the backside.

"Look, Zen, it's been days, and I haven't been able to get inside. You have to give me more information than just 'look for a White Knight.'"

"But that's all I have!" Zen screamed though the phone. She could hear his heavy breathing and his swallow to suppress his anger.

She lowered her voice. "If you let me talk to Jo, we could figure something out."

"You want to talk to her? Okay." Zen turned on the video phone. He grabbed Jo's hair and smashed her face onto the screen of the phone. "Do you see her now? Talk away. You girls can figure things out, right?"

Madeline caught a glimpse of Zen's face, which was burning red with fury. Jo's eyes were dazed, and her forehead was bruised. Jo bit her lips and looked into the screen. Madeline knew Jo wouldn't cry.

"You hurt her, you bastard. You told me you wouldn't hurt her if I found your stupid avatar!" Madeline roared.

"But you found *nothing*!" Zen screamed.

CHAPTER 3

"He didn't hurt me, Madeline. I tried to run and fell down the stairs. Should have taken my stupid heels off." Jo smiled weakly.

A tear rolled down Madeline's cheek. Jo was barely five foot two, and she always wore those impossibly high heels. Madeline couldn't understand why she was so conscious about her height. Jo was gorgeous. She was a brilliant computer game designer, but no one could peg her as a nerd. Madeline wiped her tear and smiled back.

"You sure you're okay?"

"I'm fine. You take care of yourself, Madeline."

"I can't get the blue dots to work, Jo. Can you tell me what the game is about? What am I looking for?"

Jo was about to say something, but Zen yanked her off the phone. "All you have to do is to find out who plays with Jo using the name White Knight. You've seen the game—and the player. You should be able to tell who the guy is in real life. I told you he works for the LeBlancs and has been playing from that building. You don't have to go in. Just wait him out."

"Do you understand that LeBlanc Pharmaceuticals is a global company that employs millions of people?"

"But I gave you the *precise* location!"

"I told you, it's like a military barrack. I used my journalist credentials to ask for an interview with their PR department . . ."

"And?"

"The waiting list is a month."

"I don't have a month. I give you three days."

"It's not possible . . ."

"I don't give a shit. If I don't get this done in time, I'll be dead. But I'm not going down alone. I can guarantee you that. I'll send you more info as soon as I have it. But three days is all the time you've got."

Zen hung up.

Madeline slid down to the floor and curled up next to the sofa. She let the tears fall freely. She could fall apart right here, right now. Nobody knew, and nobody cared. Jo was her family—the only family Madeline had ever known. She had taken her in and had shared her family with Madeline unconditionally. Jo's parents had never once asked Madeline about her own family—they knew she didn't have one. Otherwise, she would've had to tell them that she had come in a basket, abandoned on the front porch of some random house.

Her teeth chattered, and her body shook with the chill. She couldn't remember the last time she'd eaten or slept.

At the corner of the room, the fireplace stood cold and empty. She had forgotten to start the fire.

A shadow hovered at the window and tripped over the potted plant at the front door, but Madeline had drifted to sleep and heard nothing.

A piece of paper slid under her door.

A crash woke Madeline. She jumped up to her feet, panting.

Then she let out a sigh of relief. She had kicked the side table in her sleep, and the vase on top of the table had crashed to the floor.

Madeline checked the clock. She must have passed out for the night. It was just past five in the morning. She glanced out the window without any hope of seeing the winter sun at this hour. Madeline went to the kitchen to make herself a strong mug of coffee and to find something with which to clean up the broken vase.

A short moment later, she settled in front of her computer and stared at the mountain of documentation she had researched about LeBlanc Pharmaceuticals.

Secrets.

That was the conclusion she had drawn. Not that she couldn't find any information. On the contrary, there was too much information. Ten years of experience in journalism had taught her that the information about the LeBlancs was only a facade. Even the underground information revealed nothing about the company that they didn't want the public to know.

The LeBlanc family was filthy rich — and extremely private.

Madeline had to congratulate herself after hours of searching. She found one picture of the current head of the family, Ciaran LeBlanc. One lousy picture. The picture must have come from a very keen stalker. It was taken from a distance, and the scene it showed was reflected on a traffic monitoring mirror in a car park.

Judging by the proportion of the cars and guards around him, Madeline speculated that Ciaran was tall and well-built, but on the slender side.

Young, she mused, and maybe long hair. The picture was so distorted that Madeline wasn't sure she would have recognized Ciaran if she met him in the flesh.

She drew imaginary lines with her finger around Ciaran's face, trying to make out the part that the poor quality image didn't catch.

Then she glanced at the corner of the door, on the floor, and saw the note.

Madeline picked the note up.

It read, "Hyde Park."

CHAPTER 4

Madeline stretched for her morning run and winced at how stiff her body felt after slacking off for a week. Hyde Park was just around the corner from her place. *Had Zen wanted to tip her off as to where the LeBlancs lived?* She doubted that.

There were residential areas in Hyde Park, but she couldn't imagine the LeBlancs in these apartments, regardless of how exclusive they were. Madeline speculated that members of the LeBlanc family lived in castles in secret highlands.

She jiggled a container of self-defense spray in her pocket to ensure it was secured and within easy reach, then headed to the park.

The fog was as thick as clouds. Madeline could hardly see more than ten feet in front of her. She kept to the left, but then by habit drifted over to the right. Suddenly right in front of her, a man emerged from the fog like a warrior. Late thirties. Tall. At least six foot three, she would guess, with a slender build and well-toned muscles covered attractively in fair English skin. His thick, black hair almost touched his shoulders. His strong face, the face of a dark angel, looked straight ahead before it registered the coming motion. His eyes . . . Madeline was sure that it was his eyes that caused such an electrifying reaction in her body. Dark, smoky gray eyes. Intense, captivating, and striking.

Because Madeline had spent so much time evaluating the beauty of the human being in front of her, she didn't have any time to adjust her speed or steer herself away from the imminent collision. She would have been knocked off her feet and landed on her backside if he hadn't grabbed her.

"Goddamn it, don't you look when you run, Ciaran?"

The words were out before she could edit them. She had called his name, which meant she had to think with lightning speed right now to explain herself—to explain that she was not a stalker. Her thoughts ran rampant. She could tell him it wasn't him she was after, she wanted his company. No. She didn't want his company, she needed the guy who worked in his company. Hmm . . . but that wouldn't explain how she knew his name. Maybe she should tell him she's a psychic? No again. That would be a lie, and it wouldn't go down well. Her thoughts tangled in a mushy mess, and she felt as if her face was on fire.

Ciaran released Madeline after a swivel to balance the running momentum so that they both regained their footing. "Excuse me!" he said.

"Sorry, it was my fault. I should have kept right — no, I mean left."

"Is that an offense to run on a wrong side of a pedestrian path in a public park in New York?"

She wanted to swoon with the sexy British accent, but her suspicion had gotten a better judgment of her. Madeline narrowed her eyes. "How do you know I'm from New York?"

"Your accent gave it away. I have a lot of business dealings in New York. I can tell." Ciaran grinned.

Her heart skipped a beat when she saw that grin. *For pity's sake, you're thirty-three, not a teenager, Madeline. Focus.*

Ciaran drank from his bottle water and sat down on the bench. "I don't think my name is written on my forehead."

"Talk to your PR department. I'm the reporter who's been bugging them for the past few days to get an interview. Of course I know your name." That was lame, she thought. Ciaran didn't have a public profile, and she couldn't even get a decent picture of him. But she couldn't think of anything else, so she settled with the statement.

Ciaran nodded politely, and waited.

"Oh, I'm Madeline Roux, from *The Trumpet*." Madeline reached her hand out for a handshake.

"*The Trumpet*?"

She didn't need to look at Ciaran's face to see his expression. "Oh, we're certainly not the *New York Times* or anything . . ."

"I beg your pardon. I didn't mean to offend . . ." He stood up quickly from the bench to return the handshake before she withdrew her hand.

Madeline laughed. "You have to do a lot better than that to offend me. We're young, small, and not a mainstream magazine. Of course you've never heard of us."

Ciaran smiled. "How off-stream are you?"

"Well, let's say we're just a bit quirky in our approach to serious issues."

Ciaran murmured, "Ah, interesting! So you don't just blow the whistle, you blow the whole magnificent trumpet to the glory!"

Madeline laughed. "You've got it, Ciaran!"

She suddenly realized that she hadn't laughed for days. It felt good. But it was much too friendly. Madeline tilted her head to look behind Ciaran. He turned, looking in the same direction.

"What are you looking for?"

"Bodyguards."

Ciaran looked at Madeline blankly. Then he just laughed.

"You think I'd have bodyguards with me when I go running? Who do you think I am? A prince?"

"Practically," Madeline muttered.

"I beg your pardon?" His smile faded.

"What do you expect people to think? Your family isn't media friendly. Your company has more security than the military. Nobody knows anything about your family. It is more difficult to approach you than it is to make an appointment to see the Queen!"

"Well, that's because the Queen has to answer to her people. We don't have to answer to anyone."

"Or you'd have everyone answer to you?"

Ciaran lowered his voice. "We have money. But we don't bribe or bully anyone. I don't care for my family being judged because we want our privacy." Ciaran jammed his hands in his pockets, waiting for Madeline's response.

She cursed herself. "I'm sorry. It's just been very hard to get in touch with you. I mean with your PR department. It's almost impossible, and my boss isn't happy at all about my progress."

Ciaran nodded. "What did *The Trumpet* want to talk to our PR department about? You came all the way from New York—it couldn't be a minor issue."

"Nothing serious, really. I suggested the topic. LeBlanc Pharmaceuticals is a very successful business. I'm sure the media has made the most of what they could. But for me, behind that business success is always the people. I always find your family . . . intriguing."

Ciaran smiled. "You think we have something to hide?"

"No, I think you have a lot to show. I'd like to have a bit of what you're willing to show."

Ciaran paused for a brief moment then nodded. "So is it my family or my family's business that you're interested in?"

She looked into Ciaran's eyes. They were intense now, deep gray and mysteriously serious.

"Both."

He shook his head. "You have only one option."

"Your family."

A slight smile crossed Ciaran's face. "Then you can interview me. I will represent my family. Would tomorrow night be convenient? Over dinner?"

"What? Of course! Dinner?"

"That's the only time I can manage."

Madeline nodded.

Ciaran smiled. "Seven p.m. at One Hyde Park. I'm looking forward to it. Goodbye for now, Madeline." Ciaran nodded a goodbye and turned to walk away.

"Why? Your family has never talked to the media before."

Ciaran turned around, sending Madeline a look that made her stomach quiver. "Simply because I'd like to see more of you!" he said.

Then he walked away and disappeared into the fog.

CHAPTER 5

Madeline's internal clock woke her in the morning—it seemed she had adjusted to the time difference. She didn't have many hours of sleep, but they were good and solid hours, enough to get her going and be prepared. Tonight was her chance to end this and put her life back to normal.

Was that all she wanted with the dinner? Had she thought about Ciaran at all?

She got off the bed, giving herself a mental slap whenever her brain wandered in Ciaran's direction. She needed to stay focused and plan for the night.

She should have chosen the business rather than the family when Ciaran gave her the options. But the man headed the family *and* ran the business. He could give her the exact information she needed. If she had gone with the business option, then she might have ended up with one of the minions whose job was to withhold information from her.

Madeline made herself a cup of coffee and stopped that stream of thought. There was no point rationalizing a past action that she couldn't reverse anyway.

Her response to Ciaran in the park hadn't been optimal. But she was a woman, and his physical attraction was undeniable. *Hell, he was like a magnet!* Mental slap.

Madeline tucked at her hair, pulling it back into a ponytail and putting herself into active working mode. Her phone rang. Paul's voice squeaked through from the other end of the line when Madeline picked up.

"Here you are, still on the planet. Thank God. You can't just go poof and let me handle everything, Maddie!"

Paul was co-editor with Madeline at *The Trumpet*. His task was to add a feminine touch to the magazine. Balance the scales, he always said, as Madeline had made the magazine quite 'boyish.' Paul was a decent writer and a good guy in the industry, as far as Madeline concerned.

"A girl is entitled to a vacation, Paul!"

"I'm so glad that you finally realize you're a girl! Yes, you can take a vacation. But you have to give me some notice in advance of more than, say, half an hour!

Also, I can take care for your half-finished stories, but not your half-eaten slop, half-finished carrot rubber, and half-decent boyfriend."

"First, the slop is homemade lasagna, and you're lucky to have half of it. Second, the carrot cake is from Jo's brother's one-of-a-kind bakery, and he specifically baked it for me. So you're welcome to have it, and I'll thank them on your behalf. Third, Stephen is not a half-decent man. He's better than a lot of guys I know."

"Oh, so Stephen is your boyfriend now, is he?"

"Who were you talking about?"

"Not Stephen, apparently! A bold guy. Shuffling through your desk like a thief. Took off when I called out. Be careful, Maddie. I think you might have a stalker . . . and that's a best-case scenario."

Madeline felt a pinch of worry. A dozen what-if scenarios flew through her mind. "Are you okay?" she asked Paul. "I'm sorry if this worries you."

"No, I'm all right," Paul said.

"You want me to call Stephen? He's a cop. He could do something about this."

"No, no," Madeline assured him. "I can handle this. Give me a few days. I'll sort it out, I promise. Let me know if anything else happens. Hey . . . how about you work from home for a few days?"

Paul chuckled. "Really, Maddie?"

"Yeah, really," Madeline said. "Just do that for me, will you? I'll talk to you later. I'll explain more. Everything. Okay?"

Paul reluctantly agreed and hung up the phone.

Madeline called Zen. He switched on the video phone when he picked up the call. His sleazy smile flashed on the screen.

"Miss me?"

"You don't have to sniff around my workplace and freak out other people. I said I'd get the information for you, and I will." Madeline fumed.

The smile disappeared from Zen's face. "I didn't snoop around no place. Who else knows about this?"

A missed step, damn! Slow down, she warned herself.

"No, I'm just annoyed, that's all. I have a few unkind readers sending nasty notes to my paper, that's all."

"Your job sucks. Poking your nose into other people's business—you'll end up with something as big as a bomb or as little a bullet. They're both lethal, though! What have you got for me?"

"Ah . . . not much yet. Is White Knight a game or a character?"

"It's an avatar. Jesus Christ! Don't you know anything about games?"

"No, not really. I don't even know exactly how to get the information. Even if I should get inside the

LeBlanc premises, you want me just to go around asking who plays White Knight?"

Madeline could picture Zen wanting to knock his head against the wall to quell his frustration. *Maybe it was her head that he wanted to whack.* She chuckled on the inside and kept a straight face. Playing dumb was working for her at this point, so she kept at it.

Zen calmly explained, "No, don't ask directly, and don't alarm any one. All you have to do is to tell them that one computer within their premises was used to play an interactive game. Make it up. Say the game was illegal or whatever. Don't say anything about White Knight at this stage. I need a list of the real names of those who played games from that building. If you can narrow it down to the one guy who plays as White Knight, that's ideal. But I understand it might be difficult. Got it?"

Madeline nodded.

"When can I expect some results?"

"Come on, you only gave me Hyde Park. That's a residential address, not the business headquarters. How am I supposed to . . ."

"What? I didn't give you the address. I didn't know the address. Who tipped you? Who else knows about this?" Zen's face started to burn with anger.

Fuck! This is a total fuck-up. Who wrote the note? She searched frantically in her mind for an answer but found nothing.

"What happened? You better fucking tell me!" Zen yelled into the phone.

"I . . . I was . . ."

"*Tell me!*" Zen's demonic voice threatened to rip open the phone.

CHAPTER 6

The ceiling-high, double-steel door automatically slid open when Ciaran approached, revealing a vast lush office with glass windows opening to the endless horizon of the city. Before the door closed, Lindsay called from behind, "Ciaran!" and trailed into the office with a stack of paper in his hands.

Ciaran turned around. "Yes, Lindsay, did I forget to sign something?"

Lindsay Freeman was in his late thirties and had been Ciaran's right-hand man as long as Ciaran had been in business. As they were of similar age, Ciaran could talk to Lindsay almost about anything. They were good friends, and Ciaran trusted Lindsay to be the face of the business when it came to dealing with outsiders.

"You'll want to take a look at this," Lindsay said and put a computer disc on the desk.

Ciaran glanced at the disc. "Gate security? Shouldn't Robert be handling this?" He slid the disc into the computer.

"I just checked things over, and this caught my eye."

Ciaran shook his head. "You can't keep an eye on everything. Robert's a very capable man."

"No doubt about that. But I'll sleep better checking everything this week because you're here."

"I don't want to be the cause of your sleep deprivation. By the way, how are Liz and Anna?"

"Enjoying their vacation at a warm beach in Bali now." Lindsay grinned. "Anna finished her exams with good grades and wanted a vacation before entering high school."

Ciaran stopped looking at the computer monitor. "You're saying you let your wife and daughter go on a vacation by themselves because I'm here this week?"

Lindsay laughed. "Come on. I know your schedule, and work is important, Ciaran. They decided on the vacation on a whim. It's hardly my fault."

Ciaran shook his head. "When they kick you out of the house, you aren't going sleep on my couch."

The secretary knocked on the door and walked in with a tray. She put the coffee on the desk. "Double shot, no cream for you, Ciaran. Double cream for you, Lindsay." She put a plate of four small cookies on the desk. "Mom made these and insisted I take them to work for you, Ciaran. She does this every week. She thinks you're in the office nine to five, five days a week." She smiled. "I ate your cookies every other week. But today, they're all yours."

Ciaran grinned. "Butterscotch. My favorite. Thank you, Lily." He reached out for a cookie and his gaze lighted on Lily's hand. Ciaran dropped the cookies back to the plate. He stood up, walked around his desk, and kissed Lily on the cheek. "Congratulations, Sam is a very lucky guy."

Lily smiled and twirled her engagement ring around her finger. "Thank you. It was last week. We're very happy . . . Well, I'd better let you go back to work." She nodded a goodbye and exited the room. Ciaran grabbed the desk phone and ordered flowers to be sent to Lily's address. Then he looked up and saw Lindsay shaking his head.

"You haven't seen me doing this before?" Ciaran arched an eyebrow.

"I only say this as a friend. It's been such a long time since . . ."

"Don't start," Ciaran cut in with a voice so low that it almost sounded like a growl. Then he pointed at the computer monitor. "What did you want me to look at here?" As soon as Ciaran finished his question, he saw the answer. On the screen was Madeline in front of the LeBlanc Pharmaceuticals, walking right in front of a double-decker.

"You see that?" Lindsay asked.

Ciaran nodded. "Yes, I know her. That's Madeline Roux. She's a journalist from New York."

"I'm not talking about her. I'm talking about the guy."

Ciaran frowned, looking at the man dragging Madeline out of the way of the bus. "He's no random pedestrian. From this angle, he must have been stalking right at our door steps. We got the scanner data on that, right?"

"Yep, that's where the ass-kicker stuff is," Lindsay muttered.

Ciaran pulled out the keyboard and typed in the command and codes to pull up the scanner data. On the screen was the x-ray scanned data of a five hundred meter perimeter outside the gate. Ciaran was about to ask something, but Lindsay said in anticipation, "Robert kept a very tight lid on the scanner. We know it's not strictly legal. You don't have to be the only one to keep an eye on everything!" Lindsay smiled to himself as he had evened the scores with Ciaran.

Ciaran's smile faded as he stared at the monitor.

END OF SAMPLE CHAPTERS

HTTP://DNLEO.COM

Thank you for reading.

If you enjoyed reading **Dark Solar - Book Three - Maikoa**, I would appreciate it if you would help others enjoy this book, too.

<u>Recommend it.</u> Please help other readers find this book by recommending it to friends, readers' groups and discussion boards.

<u>Review it.</u> Please tell other readers why you liked this book by reviewing it wherever you purchase it. A few sentences will make a significant difference to me. If you do write a review, please send me an email at info@dnleo.com so I can thank you with a personal email.

Connect with me online:

http://dnleo.com

ALSO BY D.N. LEO
http://dnleo.com

A SHADE OF MIND
The Journey from Earth to Eudaiz
Main Characters: Ciaran, Madeline, Tadgh, and Jo

(Recommended reading in order)

1-4 Random Psychic

2-4 Forever Mortal

3-4 Elusive Beings

4-4 Imperfect Divine

—

MINDSCAPE
Main characters:

Ciaran, Madeline, Tadgh, Jo, Kyle, Hoyt, Ayana, Pete, Sizx, Lorcan, Orla

(Recommended reading in order within series, can be read in ANY order in related to other series)

Queen's Gambit

Knight & Pawn

Lone Castle

Doubled Bishops

Dead Squares

King's Endgame

—

SPECTRUM OF LIES

Main characters: Lorcan, Orla, Roy and Mori

(Recommended reading in order)

1-4 White Curse - Negotiate Death

2-4 Blue Fox - Befriend a Rogue

3-4 Indigo Stone - Cheat a Sorcerer

4-4 Red Moon - Break a Curse

—

SILVER BLOOD

Main characters:

Ciaran, Madeline, Tadgh, Jo, Caedmon, Sedna, Roy,

Mori, Zach, Mya, Lorcan and Orla

This series can be read in ANY order within the series

and in related to other series.

Virgo

Libra

Scorpio

THE GOOD DEITY

Main characters:

Main characters: Mya Portman, Zach Flynn, Leon, Kirra.

This series can be read in ANY order within the series and in related to other series.

Almost Countable

Almost Sure

Almost Everywhere

DARK SOLAR

Main characters:

Main characters: Dinah, Arik, Ciaran and Madeline

Oleander

Wolfsbane

Maikoa

COPYRIGHT

Dark Solar 3 - Maikoa
By D.N. Leo

I greatly appreciate you taking the time to read my work. Please consider leaving a review wherever you purchased the book, and refer the book to your friends.